MASQUERADE FOR LOVE

MASQUERADE FOR LOVE

•

GEORGETTE LIVINGSTON

Montlake Romance

The characters and events portrayed in this book are fictitious. Any similarity to real persons, living or dead, is coincidental and not intended by the author.

Printed in the United States of America.

Published by Montlake Romance
P.O. Box 400818
Las Vegas, NV 89140

ISBN-13: 9781477836323
ISBN-10: 1477836322

For Jeri May,
who knows all about boats and the sea

Thanks, sweet lady, for all your help
This one is for you

This title was previously published by Avalon Books; this version has been reproduced from the Avalon book archive files.

Chapter One

"You'd feel a lot better if you opened your eyes," the husky voice beside her said. "And you might consider sucking on some crushed ice."

Unaware that her discomfort was so obvious, but feeling too wretched to be personable, Katherine Callahan opened her eyes and said, "If you don't mind—" Suddenly her tongue seemed tangled in her mouth, and the rest of her words were barely audible. He was tall and slim, and was sort of folded into the seat uncomfortably. His feet, encased in tan-colored cowboy boots, were plunked out in the aisle, and he smelled like a mixture of fresh air, Ivory soap, and musk. The blue jeans and plaid flannel shirt looked new, with creases still in the shirtsleeves, and she would bet her next paycheck he had a Stetson in one of the overhead compartments. She thought about asking him if he'd left his horse parked at LAX, but bit back those words too, because she suddenly found herself lost in the depths of his shocking blue eyes. Sky blue? No. More like a field of wild cornflowers on a lazy summer day. There were little flecks of green and gold in them too, and tiny laugh lines at the outer edges. His dark hair was thick and wavy, and two elongated dimples creased his cheeks. Or was the one on the left side a scar? She wanted to take a closer look, but didn't dare, for fear he might get the wrong impression.

Groaning inwardly, Kate looked out the window at the dark, swirling clouds they'd flown into after twenty minutes in the air, and tried to concentrate on the deep drone of the jet engines. He was almost too handsome, and exactly the kind of man she had walked away from two years earlier.

"Sometimes striking up a conversation helps too," he went on. "You know, like getting into an intense debate over some significant issue, like our national economy, or the plight of the spotted owl in the Pacific Northwest versus the lumber industry. Or the sea otter versus the fishermen. Talking is supposed to take your mind off the queasiness. Of course, you could always ask the flight attendant for some Dramamine. But then we'll be landing soon, so I don't suppose it would help much. And then again, sometimes it's better to fight these kinds of things, and try to overcome them."

Kate's head began to pound. "I've never been a good flyer," she muttered finally. "Not even in good weather. Now, if you don't mind, I'd like to be left alone. That seat was empty when I got on the plane, so you must have a seat of your own somewhere."

"Right across the aisle," he drawled. "Sixteen-A. Unfortunately the gentlemen in sixteen-B is as drunk as a skunk, and wanted to use my shoulder as a pillow."

Kate looked over at the inebriated passenger, now sprawled over both seats, and sighed. They would be landing in another twenty minutes, and that would be the end of her misery, and the cowboy.

"You just try to relax now, while I go round up some ice from the flight attendant," he said, hauling his tall frame out of the seat.

After he'd gone, the scent of him lingered, adding to Kate's discomfort. It brought to mind wide-open spaces, leather saddles, horseflesh, and Michael Downs, who had said he loved her, but who had loved his cattle ranch more. On the night of their terrible (and last) fight, after she announced she was going to keep her job after they were married, he had announced no wife of his was going to work outside the home. Her job was at the ranch, doing "wifely duties," and being there for him at the end of each drudgery-filled day. He'd then reminded her it wasn't easy making a cattle ranch a paying proposition, and a few calluses were to be expected. The only thing was, he expected her to have calluses too, when she wasn't cooking, cleaning, and having babies. Not that she hadn't been aware of the difficulties involved in becoming a rancher's wife. Her mother had been one for thirty-five years. But the difference had been her wonderful father, who put his wife first, and then the ranch. Their love had been, and still was, a beautiful thing to behold—caring and giving in every way.

"And *that*" she told her sister a few days after the breakup, "is what I get for falling in love with a thoughtless, macho, insensitive cowboy. The next important man in my life is going to be civilized, respect women and the way things are today, and he's going to love me for who I am, and understand I have needs too."

Leanna had snorted. "You'd better come back to earth, Kate, because you're not going to find a guy like that in or anywhere near Peach Springs, Arizona."

"*You* did," Kate had retaliated.

"Johnny is the exception," Leanna returned. "But I'm not going to divorce him so you can have him."

Kate had hugged her sister and grinned. "Well, the least you could do is share."

Three weeks later, after listening to her parents list one hundred and one reasons why she would never, *ever* be happy in a big city, though they offered her their support in every way, Kate quit her job as a clerk in Ballard's Dry Goods, and flew to Los Angeles, because her disastrous relationship with Michael hadn't been the only disappointment in her life. She'd gone to college to pursue her dream of becoming a journalist, and had ended up clerking in a store because there weren't any jobs requiring her skills in Peach Springs, Arizona, other than with the local newspaper, and it was a family business. No outsiders allowed.

That had been two years ago. Now, she had a cozy, convenient apartment in North Hollywood, and a job as a copy editor with *Ms. California,* a chic women's publication. Admittedly there were times when she missed a quieter way of life, and the beauty that went along with miles and miles of open grazing land and the purple-hued mountains beyond, but she had never regretted her decision. Unfortunately, she was no closer to finding a meaningful relationship than before, because all the men she'd met were either too young, too old, married, or glitzy rich, which created a whole new set of problems.

"Miss, would you like something to drink?"

Kate looked up at the smiling flight attendant and the cart brimming with bottles and cans, thought about the cowboy on his search for ice, and nodded. "Champagne, and a glass of crushed ice." This was her first vacation in two years, after all, and she'd nearly hocked her soul for a glamorous wardrobe and five nights at the Fairmont Hotel on Nob Hill. The past was behind her, and no matter what the future held, she planned to enjoy every minute in San Francisco.

Kate sipped champagne from a plastic glass, crunched on ice, and felt better immediately. Until she found herself thinking about the cowboy's remarkable blue eyes, and the way his white teeth had glistened in contrast to his deeply tanned skin. Long fingers too, and…Kate shook her head, forcing herself to think about all the things she planned to do and see in the "city by the bay."

She was softly humming the strains to "I Left My Heart in San Francisco" and wondering if her hotel room would have a view of the bay, when the cowboy returned with a plastic cup filled with ice.

"Sorry it took so long," he said, settling into the seat, "but a young lady in twenty-five-A was having some problems. You know, first flight, traveling alone, and scared to death…" He stopped in mid-breath when he saw the champagne and ice on her tray, and shrugged. "Guess I must have been gone longer than I thought."

"It was your idea to go after the ice," Kate said coolly. "Though I am curious—do you make a habit of trying to comfort people in distress?"

He gave her a charming wink. "Only pretty ladies. I can tell you're feeling better. You've got some color in your cheeks."

"It's the champagne, not the ice," Kate retorted, wondering why the thought of him comforting some other stressed-out female bothered her.

A few minutes later, Kate found herself glaring up at the pretty flight attendant too, who had paused, after picking up the empty cups, to give the cowboy a dimpled, eyelash-fluttering smile. At that point, Kate wondered if she was losing her mind. Who cared if he was a flirt, or who flirted with him, or how many "pretty ladies" he wanted to help?

Relieved when the captain announced they were making their final approach, Kate buckled up, closed her eyes, and hung on. It was going to be a bumpy landing because San Francisco was in the middle of a blinding storm.

The cowboy's warm hand covered hers for a brief moment, and his vibrant, velvety-sounding voice was very close to her ear when he said, "Count to twenty and it will be over."

Kate counted to fifty-five. When she

opened her eyes, most of the passengers had gotten off the plane, and the cowboy was gone.

Kate hurried toward the luggage carousel in the terminal, bucking the incoming wet and bedraggled travelers, and then slowed her steps. He was a few feet ahead of her, sauntering along with a knapsack over his shoulder. She noted the cowboy hat perched on his head, and felt a tug of satisfaction. Once a cowboy, always a cowboy. She also noted his height. He was much taller than she'd imagined. Maybe six-three or -four, and his shoulders were very broad. When a pretty brunette woman brushed by him and smiled, he returned her smile and tipped his hat.

Kate slowed her pace even more, praying he didn't have any luggage and would keep right on going. But he turned with the crowd and headed for the carousel. Now she prayed that his luggage would be first, so he would be on his way. Or that hers would be last. A long time ago, she suddenly remembered, her grandmother had told her God didn't answer prayers if you were thinking evil thoughts. Out came her luggage, clattering down the chute.

She tucked herself in behind a tall man in a black topcoat and waited. And waited. Finally, the man who had been her protective wall moved forward to retrieve his luggage. To her dismay there was now only one person left at the carousel, and it was the cowboy.

He turned around, saw her, and smiled. "Looks like we have the same taste in luggage."

Exasperated, Kate looked down at the nearly matching two-piece sets of tan, soft-sided luggage. *Wouldn't you know?* she said to herself. She'd purchased her set during a blue-light special because she hadn't been able to afford the designer luggage she really wanted. Susan James, her best friend and coworker at *Ms. California,* had promptly said, "Better mark your name tags in big black letters, Kate. One out of ten people in California owns luggage like that."

"Got mine at a blue-light special," the

cowboy said casually. "These days, it pays to save a buck."

He pulled both sets off the carousel and managed to tuck one piece under each arm, grasp the handles of the other two, and ask, "Going into the city?"

She nodded.

"Me too. Somebody meeting you?"

"No…. I'm getting a cab."

"Me too," he said, heading toward the exit.

Kate had no choice but to follow him.

Because of the foul weather, cabs were at a premium, so by the time the cowboy whistled one down, they were both soaking wet. After the luggage had been deposited in the trunk, he told the cabdriver to head for the city, and held the door open. When she made no move to get in, he said, "You might be in for a long wait before the next cab. Could catch your death in weather like this."

Kate was too miserable to argue. But it didn't matter. In less than an hour, she would be in her hotel room, and that would definitely be the end of it!

Kate gave him an aggravated glance, and slid into the back seat.

After they were on their way, the cowboy wiped his face with his shirtsleeve and grinned. “Something tells me I should have gone on to Blue Sky and saved this trip for another day.”

Aware that her expensive new dress was ruined, and that her mascara was probably running, Kate fumbled in her purse for a tissue and muttered, “Blue Sky?”

“Montana. I own a sheep ranch. Of course, the spring thaw comes late to that part of the country, so it’s probably still under ten feet of snow. But I’ll take snow over this liquid sunshine any day of the week.”

A sheep rancher? Wonderful! Biting back all the things she wanted to say, she muttered again, “So why didn’t you? Go on to Montana, I mean.”

“A friend of mine in San Francisco is ill, and I thought I’d better pay him a visit.”

Kate used the tissue to wipe her face. “So you’ve been vacationing in L.A.?”

"I had business in L.A. You?"

"I live in L.A., and decided to spend a few days in San Francisco shopping. Of course, I would rather be on my way to Paris, but I didn't have the time."

Wondering if the cowboy had noted the sudden flush to her cheeks, the result of her bold-faced lie, Kate turned away from him and tried to see through the fogged-up window. Finally, she gave up, and drew a scowling face on the glass with her fingertip, a reflection of her mood.

When small rivulets of water gave the face a wash of vertical wrinkles, the cowboy chuckled huskily. "I'd say mine's better."

She looked over at the outline he had drawn on his window, and felt an involuntary smile crease the corners of her mouth. "It's a dog."

"Nope. It's supposed to be a sheep. Where are you staying?"

"The Fairmont Hotel…." She wanted to bite off her tongue the minute the words were out of her mouth. She easily could have said, "We'll let the cabbie take you to your destination first, and I'll go on from there," which would have given him a pretty good indication that she didn't want him to know where she was staying.

"First stop, the Fairmont Hotel," he told the cabbie, adding, "I'm headed for North Beach."

After he'd given the cabbie the address in North Beach, white teeth flashed in another effervescent smile. She decided the drive would be a lot easier if he would stop smiling. Or talking. He also had an easygoing way about him, and she found it more than disconcerting. She planned to keep a journal of her vacation, and mentally made her first entry:

> *The flight was awful, made even worse by a dark-haired cowboy with riveting blue eyes, who obviously makes a habit of trying to comfort damsels in distress. We landed at San Francisco International in the middle of a blinding storm. I had to share a cab into the city with the infuriating cowboy. He's a sheep*

rancher, no less, and bought his luggage at a blue-light special. If somebody asked me to describe his eyes, I don't think I could. Paul Newman? No, not blue enough. The sky? Well, maybe, after a summer storm....

When the cabbie and the cowboy struck up a conversation about Montana, Kate breathed a sigh of relief. It freed her to relax and mentally go over her itinerary. Susan loved San Francisco, but hadn't been much help. Coffeehouses, delicatessens, comedy clubs, and the nightclub scene at midnight were not on Kate's agenda.

The travel agent had been much more helpful. "San Francisco in the spring—how marvelous! Shopping in Union Square, and the plays and the opera. Oh, and you'll find flower vendors on every corner." Kate didn't think vendors would be selling flowers now, with the storm assaulting the city, but there were other things to do and see, and the storm wouldn't last forever.

By the time they reached the heart of

the city and Market Street, the rain had stopped, lifting her spirits, even though the sky was still darkly ominous. She started picking out points of interest she'd read about in the brochures the travel agent had given her, and perched on the edge of her seat.

"I take it this is your first visit to San Francisco?" the cowboy asked.

She'd almost forgotten he was beside her. Almost. "Why would you think that?"

"Because of the excitement I can see in your eyes. The expectation. And I meant that as a compliment."

Of course he did. Men like that were always free with compliments, but fell short when it came to a woman's feelings. Like Michael, who could tell her that her hair looked like spun gold touched by the setting sun in one breath, then hand her a shovel and tell her to muck out the barn before he took the next. "I've been here too many times to count," she lied again, and felt the tips of her ears burn.

She hung on as the cabbie wildly maneuvered around traffic and careened up the hills, and felt light-headed. It was his driving, she told herself. *Not* because the cowboy's thigh was pressed against hers. Or that the wet smell of him reminded her of a garden full of summer flowers.

At one point, the cabbie had to slam on the brakes, and the cowboy put out an arm to keep her from pitching forward. She could feel the warmth from him, and an unwelcome ripple of awareness.

When they finally pulled up in front of the Fairmont Hotel, Kate sighed with relief. And oh, what a grand old hotel it was, with its canopied entrance and rich history. Unfortunately, the cowboy was spoiling the picture. She had dreamed about this moment, of being greeted by a smiling doorman, and being whisked into luxury. Instead, the cowboy had waved the doorman away, and was hauling her luggage out of the trunk.

Kate got out and shivered as the cold wind whipped through her damp clothing. But her voice was firm when she said, "The cab driver should be doing that, and the hotel should be taking care of my luggage."

The cowboy shrugged, and whistled through his teeth for the departing doorman. He followed that tactless maneuver with a casual, "Suit yourself."

Kate fumbled in her purse, trying to find the two twenty-dollar bills she had tucked away for cab fare, but could only find a crumpled five.

The cowboy stopped her by placing a hand on her arm. "This is on me. I'd be paying for the cab anyway, so save your money for your shopping spree.

"By the way, my name is Michael Gordon. And you are…."

Michael! Wonderful! "I don't think—"

"We've shared a cab and a dismal spring afternoon," he said, grinning mischievously. "So humor me."

And he was arrogant along with everything else. "Katherine Ann Devlin," she mumbled. She had no idea why she had used her mother's maiden name, but felt too befuddled to sort it out. What was done was done.

"Katherine Ann Devlin," he said, as though he was tasting it on the tip of his tongue. "It's a beautiful name. It suits you. Enjoy your vacation, Katie lady."

Kate gritted her teeth and headed for the hotel. At the entrance, she chanced a glance over her shoulder. Michael Gordon was leaning against the cab. Because of the distance, she couldn't see his eyes, but she could feel them on her as she walked into the lobby.

Chapter Two

On the short drive between the Fairmont Hotel and Bonini's Bakery and Delicatessen in North Beach, Michael tried to sort out his feelings. Admitting he was attracted to Katherine Ann Devlin was the hardest part, because she was exactly the kind of woman he'd vowed to stay away from, after his disastrous experience with Monica Lang. Polished, professional, all glitter and glamor, and encased in ice. Yet there was something about her that didn't ring true. First and foremost, why would a woman of her caliber be lugging around cheap luggage?

Or lose her lustrous poise, if only for a brief moment? When she'd drawn the face on the cab window, he'd had a hard time believing what he was seeing. And then there was the eagerness she had displayed when they'd reached the city, even though she said she'd been to San Francisco many times. And he couldn't forget her wonderful smile either, when he'd attempted to draw a sheep on his window. It had broken through her icy exterior like a ray of sunlight on a dark winter day. Nor could he overlook the biggest question of all: would she have been so cold and indifferent toward him if he had been sitting beside her dressed in his one good suit? Or if he had introduced himself as Dr. Michael Gordon, head of the Neurosurgery Department at Mt. Zion Hospital? Or would she have run with it, like Monica, thinking only of the prestige and the dollar signs he represented?

When the cabdriver pulled up to the corner of Union and Columbus, Michael paid the fare and hurried into the store, pushing Katherine Ann Devlin out of his mind. Angelo had taken a turn for the worse, and his dear friend should be his only concern.

"Maria!" he called, breathing in the wonderful aromas that always permeated the bakery and deli.

Maria Bonini poked her nose out of the storeroom, saw Michael, and rushed into his arms.

He gave the plump, dark-haired little lady a giant hug before he said, "That's some greeting. I've only been gone two days."

"I know, and we were resigned to the fact you wouldn't be around for three weeks while you were in Blue Sky, but then Angelo felt dizzy, and I got so worried…." She looked up at Michael, and shook her head. "I shouldn't have called. The dizziness is over, and—"

"You did the right thing," Michael interrupted. "Angelo just had major surgery, and we can't be too careful. If anything, I'm to blame for planning the trip to Blue Sky now. A month or so down the road would've been a lot better."

Maria clucked her tongue. "And you

shouldn't have to put your life on hold because of us." A dimple creased her cheek as her dark eyes took in his clothing. "You make a very handsome cowboy, Dr. Gordon. Trina is going to fall in love with you all over again."

Michael gave her a crooked grin. "She's married and pregnant, and I'm almost old enough to be her father."

"Almost, but not quite. She is in love with John Wayne too. And Clint Eastwood."

At that moment, Trina, the Boninis' beautiful twenty-year-old daughter, carefully made her way down the stairs and then rushed into Michael's arms. "I thought I heard your voice!" she squealed. "Just look at you! You're gorgeous in cowboy clothes!"

Michael patted her belly. "And look at you! I've only been gone two days, and you've gotten bigger."

Trina, who was a carbon copy of her mother, giggled. "Think I'll make it to my due date?"

Michael shook his head. "That's six weeks away. I don't know, sweetheart.

It's going to be close. Shall we go upstairs so I can check on your papa?"

Trina rolled her eyes. "Papa isn't happy. He's angry because Mama called you. He says you should be in Blue Sky, taking a well-deserved vacation."

"Blue Sky can wait," Michael said, climbing the stairs two at a time.

"And so can I," Angelo Bonini grunted from the landing. "My wife and daughter make too much of nothing."

Angelo had rolled his wheelchair out of their living quarters, and gave one of the chair arms an angry smack. "And this is something else that I can do without."

"Orders are orders," Michael said, pushing the wheelchair into the warm, comfortable living groom. "You've been told you are to stay in the wheelchair until you need a haircut, because we sure wouldn't want you falling and bumping your head, would we?"

Angelo scratched around the bandage, and sighed. "I feel so helpless, and it's too much for Maria to have to do all the work."

Maria walked into the room behind them, pulled down the shades against the storm, turned on the lights, and announced, “Do you hear me complaining?”

“Did you put the CLOSED sign in the store window?” Angelo asked his wife.

Maria threw up her hands. “And that is something else. He thinks I haven’t a brain in my head. Of course I put the sign in the window. I also have a pot of vegetable soup on the stove, and I remembered to scrape the carrots. Come along, Trina, and help me in the kitchen.”

After the women left the room, Angelo shook his head. “She forgot to bring up a loaf of bread.”

Michael chuckled. “I’ll get it later. Why the bandage, Angelo? Your incision is well healed, and—”

Angelo raised a beefy hand. “It’s better to look at with the bandage covering it. I take it off at night before I go to bed.”

“Your wife and daughter have seen the incision,” Michael reminded him. “They know what it looks like.”

“I don’t keep it covered for them. I keep it covered for me. I don’t want to be reminded of that night I almost died. Right now, it is so good to be alive. I know I'm cranky and impatient, but I'm anxious to get back to the business of living. Really living." He eyed Michael intently. "And you, my good friend, should be having dinner tonight with your mama in Blue Sky, Montana."

"I called her from L.A. and said I'd be a few days late. When I'm convinced you're not going to drop dead in a heartbeat, I'll be on my way."

"Then I suppose you plan to stay here until you're convinced?"

"If you mean here with you instead of going home, you're right."

"You'll have to sleep on that lumpy mattress in the spare bedroom."

"I'll sleep on the lumpy couch in the living room, if I have to, or even on the floor. I went through a lot to close up my house, and I see no point in having to do it again. Besides, if my neighbors got a look at me dressed like this, they'd probably call the cops."

Angelo grunted. "By now, I would

think they would be used to your casual ways of dressing. What's the difference?"

"Forget it," Michael said, taking a small leather bag out of his tote. "You're not going to get rid of me, and that's that."

After Michael examined Angelo, he closed up the bag and said, "Maria said you were dizzy?"

"It only lasted a few minutes. She over-reacted."

"Well, everything seems to be working properly, though your blood pressure is a little high. Have you been drinking too much wine?"

Angelo looked away. "You operated and brought me back from that black hole called death, Michael. I can't thank you enough for that, but don't tell me how to live my life."

"I'm not only going to tell you how to live your life, I'm going to make sure you follow through. One glass of wine before dinner, and one with. That's it."

Angelo grinned slyly. "My Maria is in the kitchen fixing dinner."

Michael sighed, and went to the sideboard to pour two glasses of wine. He handed one to Angelo, and they touched glasses. "To life," Michael said. "You'll always be a crotchety, hard-nosed old man, but I still love you."

"And you've always been the one man who can set me straight. But I still love you." His grin was wide. "You sure look different in those cowboy clothes."

"Feel different too. Now, all I have to do is learn to ride a horse."

Angelo's laughter was hearty, and filled the room. "Monica was always complaining about the way you dressed. Thought you should dress like a doctor instead of bum. Well, she should see you now."

Michael wasn't upset by the comment, but it did bring to mind Katherine Ann Devlin, and how she might have reacted to him had she known he was a doctor instead of a sheep rancher. In retrospect, he had absolutely no idea why he hadn't clarified things when he'd had the chance, though he supposed it was because of Monica. On the other hand, it didn't matter. She was simply a beautiful woman he'd met on the flight from L.A. End of story.

But it wasn't the end of the story, because a little later, while they sat around the dinner table enjoying Maria's soup and crusty slices of bread, Katherine Ann Devlin crept into the conversation. And by the time Michael had finished describing her, and told them about the brief time they'd spent together on the plane and in the cab, Trina was teasing him unmercifully, and the Boninis' eyes danced with merriment. Most of the time, the Boninis didn't agree on anything and, as a result, they spent a lot of time haggling. But they were always together when it came to affairs of the heart. His heart, mostly, and they had a penchant for matchmaking. First there had been the lady from the grocery, then the fish market, and then a friend's daughter, and then one of their customer's daughters, and now Katherine Ann Devlin, the lady with the warm green eyes and cold tongue, who was a paradox at best.

* * *

After watching the eleven o'clock news, Michael said good night to Trina and the Boninis, and carried his luggage into the small bedroom off the kitchen. Although he wasn't going to unpack, he would need a few things, like his tooth-brush, shaving gear, pajamas, and a change of clothing for tomorrow, and maybe the crossword puzzle book he'd picked up in L.A.... Michael frowned. He'd placed the suitcases on the bed side by side, but one of them wasn't his! It was a little lighter in color for one thing, and the name tag—Michael groaned. Katherine Callahan. *Callahan?*

Puzzled, Michael sat down on the bed and held the plastic-encased identification tag in his hand. It was easy to see how he could have gotten the two suit-cases mixed up when he took them out of the cab, and that meant Katherine had *his* suitcase, but why had she lied to him? She'd given him a phony last name.... Or, was she married, but going by her maiden name, like so many professional women did? Well, if she was married, she wasn't wearing a wedding ring. He remembered her long, tapered fingers, void of jewelry or nail polish He shook his head. In any event, it was too late to do anything about the mixup tonight. First thing tomorrow morning, he would take the suitcase to the hotel, make the exchange, apologize, and that would be the end of it. No harm done, unless the suitcase he had contained her toiletries and nightclothes. That might ruffle her up a bit.

Michael smiled slightly at the thought, but the humor was short-lived when he remembered a comment his sister had made one time while she was packing for a trip to Mexico. If any of her suitcases went astray, or was lost, stolen, or rerouted, she could only hope and pray it wouldn't be the one with her cosmetics, toiletries, undergarments, and nightclothes, the things she felt were absolutely essential to any woman on a trip.

With that thought in mind, and trying to convince himself it was the *only* reason to open her suitcase, because if it did contain those kinds of intimate things he would have to take the suitcase to the hotel right away, Michael took out a pocketknife and went to work on the lock. It didn't take long. But he didn't find cosmetics and intimate apparel, only an empty journal and several articles of clothing, which meant she wouldn't be needing them until tomorrow, and he could stick to his original plan.

Michael picked up the soft sea-green silk, noted the price tag attached to the sleeve, and frowned. Next came the black crepe, a few casual dresses, and the various skirts, pants, sweaters, and blouses, all with the sales tags firmly attached. Had she purchased them and packed so quickly that she'd forgotten to remove them? Or….

Maria was still in the kitchen, putting away the dinner dishes, when Michael trotted out, carrying the green dress. He explained the mixup a little sheepishly, and why he'd opened the suitcase, and then asked, "So what do you think, Maria? Is it possible she packed so quickly, she didn't have time to remove the tags, or…."

Maria gave Michael an impish grin.

"Or did she do what I did that time we went to Italy, when I couldn't afford a new wardrobe, and left the tags on all the garments so I could return the ones I didn't wear when I got home? If that's the case, Michael, I would say the lady made this trip on a very tight budget, but worked very hard to give you the opposite impression."

Michael absently rubbed the green silk against his cheek. "But why would she do that?"

Maria shrugged. "Maybe she wanted to create a little mystery, or a fantasy. Weren't you doing the same thing, claiming to be a sheep rancher from Montana?"

"It's not the same thing, Maria. My motives were purely innocent."

"And hers weren't?"

"She gave me a phony name. The identification tag on the suitcase says Callahan, not Devlin."

"So if that bothers you so much, ask her about it when you return the suitcase. If she wants you to know, she'll tell you. Meanwhile, you might want to ask yourself why any of this is bothering you." She waved a hand. "It is a simple mixup that can be easily corrected. Yes?"

Maria's dark eyes were filled with humor, and Michael scowled. "Yes, Maria, it can be, and it will be, first thing tomorrow morning."

"Then best you set your alarm clock," she teased. "You wouldn't want to oversleep."

Kate's hotel room was lovely, done in shades of cream and burgundy, with a king-size bed, two chairs, and a small desk. She also had a spectacular view overlooking Telegraph Hill. But all that was lost to Kate now, as she stared down at the larger of the two suitcases on the bed. It wasn't hers. She'd broken a nail and nearly mangled the key trying to get it open before she checked the name tag. Michael Gordon. And she could see it all. In a little while, she would receive a call from somebody at the front desk. She would be told a gentleman was in the lobby with her suitcase, because there had been a mixup. She would be expected to lug his suitcase down, or invite him up. Of course, he would be betting on the latter, and that she would be eternally grateful. So grateful, she would be putty in his hands. Big fat chance!

Angrier than she had been in a very long time, she hauled the suitcase off the bed and placed it near the door. When Michael Gordon arrived, she would have a bellman make the exchange. Meanwhile, because every piece of clothing she'd purchased for the trip was in the other suitcase, she was stuck with nightwear, an assortment of shoes and belts, undergarments, one old battered sweater, and a pair of scruffy jeans. She'd brought along the sweater and jeans so she could be comfortable in her room, but there was no way she was going to wear them anywhere else in the hotel, or out on the street. Fortunately, she'd had the foresight to pack her makeup and toiletries in a carry-on tote.

For the next hour, Kate fumed, but kept busy unpacking the few things she had, taking a shower, and trying to dry her scraggly-looking dress with a hair dryer. But the material was challis, and responded accordingly. By the time the dress was dry, size eight had turned into size five.

Frustrated beyond tears, Kate brushed out her hair, applied a fresh coat of makeup for a morale boost, and ordered room service. She had planned to eat dinner in one of the hotel's elegant restaurants. But now, because of a lunatic cowboy, she was going to have to pay twice the price, and settle for a lonely meal in front of the TV.

While she waited, she called Susan. Susan picked up the phone on the fifth ring, and sounded breathless. "Just wanted to let you know I got here in one piece," Kate said. "Is this a bad time?"

"No, of course not. I got away from the office late, that's all. And now I'm trying to decide what to wear. Todd is taking me out for pizza."

"You hate pizza."

"Uh-huh, but for a chance to go out with Todd, I'd even eat fried liver and Brussels sprouts. You sound funny, Kate. Is everything okay?"

"Everything is fine," Kate lied. "You know how I hate to fly, and we landed at San Francisco International in the middle of a storm."

"Bumpy landing, huh?"

"To say the least. But my room is lovely, and I have a wonderful view."

"Lovely, like in silk and satin and opulence beyond description?"

"No, nothing like that, but it is quite elegant."

"So, are you going to put on one of your spectacular new dresses and eat dinner in one of the hotel's spectacular restaurants?"

Unable to tell her friend the truth, Kate simply said, "Not tonight. I still feel a little queasy, so I've ordered room service."

Susan sighed. "Room service sounds wonderful. Better than pizza, even if I *am* going out with Todd. Take care, Kate, and have a great time."

Kate said that she would, rang off, and tried to swallow around the lump in her throat.

The dinner tray came and went, and Kate still hadn't heard from the front desk. Finally, at eight o'clock, she called down and explained the problem. The syrupy-voiced woman sounded genuinely concerned, and promised to "give her a jingle" the minute Mr. Gordon arrived.

But Mr. Gordon didn't arrive, and Kate feel asleep watching the eleven o'clock news.

Chapter Three

Kate overslept the next morning, and opened her eyes to bright sunlight and the ringing phone. She had been in the middle of a wonderful dream involving the cowboy, and not only felt shocked, but betrayed. How could her body and subconscious mind respond like that when she not only detested the man, but everything he stood for? "Yes, what is it?" she barked into the receiver.

"This is Mr. Morris, the front desk manager, Miss Callahan. Have you located your missing suitcase?"

"No, I haven't," Kate returned, trying

to untangle her long legs from the bedding. "Why would *I* have it? If thc man who took it returned it, *you'd* have it. I mean, you don't give out room numbers or anything, do you?"

"No, of course not," the man replied. "You're not suggesting this Mr. Gordon took your suitcase deliberately, are you? Perhaps I should call security, or the police?"

Kate ran a hand through her tousled hair and sighed. "I'm not suggesting anything at this point, Mr. Morris. And contacting the police would be a waste of time, because I haven't any information to give them."

He cleared his throat. "Well, perhaps you could give me some information? I believe you talked to Mrs. Dupont last night. I have her report in front of me now. You shared a cab with Mr. Gordon, and believe the suitcases were switched when you reached the hotel?"

"Yes, I do. Our suitcases were similar. Well, almost. Tan, soft-sided, purchased at the same store. Well, not necessarily the same store...." Aware she was sounding like a befuddled twit, and that the manager probably thought the whole incident was an innocent mistake, Kate tried again. "Mr. Gordon… Mr. Gordon tried to strike up a conversation on the plane, and then I was forced to share his cab because of the rain. He was the one who took my luggage out of the cab, and I thought perhaps he switched them deliberately, thinking it would be a way to see me later. I fully expected him to pop up downstairs with my suitcase, explain the circumstances, and…." Now she was coming off sounding arrogant, and quickly added, "I realize now, if Mr. Gordon switched our bags, it couldn't have been intentional. Too much time has gone by."

Mr. Morris pressed on. "Perhaps he hasn't had a chance to unpack, so he isn't aware of the mixup. Was there anything of value in the suitcase?"

"All my good clothes," Kate said dejectedly.

"Well, of course we can't be held responsible inasmuch as the incident didn't happen in the hotel, but we would certainly like to help you during this trying time, so if there is anything we can do, don't hesitate to let us know."

Kate hung up. There wasn't anything anybody could do. She was doomed to stay in her hotel room all week, unless.... The cowboy had given the cabbie an address, and mentioned something about North Beach and a delicatessen. Wishing she'd paid more attention, Kate squeezed her eyes shut and tried to remember. She was sure he'd said Union Street at Columbus, but she couldn't come up with an address.

Hurriedly, Kate looked up the listings for delicatessens in the dog-eared phone book, and found several on Columbus. She called all of them, but nobody had heard of Michael Gordon. While she had the phone book open, she looked up a listing for Michael Gordon. There were a lot of Gordons, but not one Michael.

Feeling so frustrated she wanted to scream, Kate eyed the cowboy's suitcase. If she could get it open, there might be something inside that would give her a clue. But what to use? A paper clip? A nail file? Obviously, it couldn't be opened with a fingernail or a key, because she'd already tried that. And then she remembered the tiny packet of miniature-sized tools in her tote, a carryover from her days in Peach Springs. Her mother had always maintained that no woman should go anywhere without a tool kit, a sewing kit, a first-aid kit, and at least two dollars in change, in the event she had to make an emergency phone call.

Kate took the tool kit out of her tote, decided on the teeny, tiny screwdriver, and went to work on the lock. It didn't take long, and when it popped open she sighed with relief.

Not surprised to see the assortment of jeans, flannel shirts, and long Johns, but a bit puzzled because it was obvious none of clothing had been worn, Kate removed each item from the suitcase, checked the pockets, and found nothing. Nothing in the suitcase pockets either, or in the large top pocket, other than a crossword puzzle book, a map of Montana, two snack-sized bags of potato chips, and a travel alarm clock.

After unceremoniously dumping everything back in the suitcase, Kate knew she couldn't sit around any longer. And so she slipped into the dress that was too short and too tight, topped it with the knock-around sweater, and called a cab. With her luck, the cowboy didn't know he had the wrong suitcase, and was halfway to Blue Sky, Montana by now. Yet she had to give this a try.

"North Beach," she told the cabdriver a few minutes later, scrunching down in the seat. Getting from her room to the lobby hadn't been bad. But after that, she'd felt every eye on her as she hurried across the cavernous, luxurious room toward the glass doors, lugging the suitcase while trying to avoid the bellmen, and clutching the sweater around her body. Size eight simply did not fit into size five.

"Where to in North Beach?" the cabdriver asked, sailing down California Street with the ease of a veteran San Francisco cabbie.

Kate clung to the seat. "Corner of Union and Columbus." Her journal was also in the missing suitcase, so she made her second mental entry:

> *Last night was a total loss because the cowboy has my suitcase containing all my beautiful clothes. Three paychecks and a huge bill at Macy's, and I'm left with underwear and grubbiest Day Two has me wearing a dress three sizes too small. If and when I find the cowboy, I'm going to cheerfully strangle him! One plus: the storm is almost over! I'm in a cab heading for North Beach, and see a few sprinkles on the window, but the sun is playing tag with the clouds, and I can see blue sky. A deep blue like the cowboy's eyes….*

Kate mentally erased the last part of the entry.

When the cabdriver finally pulled up at the curb, Kate paid him, hauled out the suitcase, and then squinted into the sunlight, trying to read the signs along the busy avenue. She held her breath when she walked by the fish market, but breathed in deeply when she reached Bonini's Bakery and Delicatessen. The aroma of freshly baked bread was wonderful! This was an establishment she hadn't phoned earlier, but then she hadn't been looking under the listing for bakeries, either.

Knowing she had to start someplace, Kate lugged the suitcase into the store. She was immediately surrounded by the marvelous smells of salami, cheese, and bread. She smiled at the small, plump, dark-haired woman behind the counter and said, "I'm looking for a cowboy. His name is Michael Gordon."

The woman's dark eyes twinkled. "You must be the pretty lady Michael met on the plane. You'll find him upstairs. Just go on up and knock on the door."

If the woman had said, "He's expecting you," Kate wouldn't have been surprised. "I'd rather have him come down here," Kate insisted.

"Ah, but he is visiting with my husband, and you know how it is when two men get together. Besides, we don't have a private line. I'd have to get a ladder, climb all the way up, and hit a broom handle on the ceiling."

Kate sighed. "You say up the stairs?"

The woman nodded. "Up the stairs and turn right. It will be the first door."

Kate struggled with the suitcase, and finally got it up the steep stairs. By the time she reached the door, her arms were shaking with fatigue. She knocked, and waited.

A pretty, dark-haired young woman, who was very pregnant, answered the door. Behind her, the cowboy was talking to a man in a wheelchair. He was still wearing jeans, but had exchanged the plaid shirt for a skintight T-shirt. Black, with yellow lettering on the back: *Don't ask. I haven't had my morning coffee.*

He turned around and raised a brow. "Well, this is a surprise. How did you find me?"

Kate put down the suitcase and swallowed, trying to ignore his golden, well-muscled arms, the flash of teeth, and the look of awareness as his blue eyes flickered over her. "You gave the address to the cabbie," she blurted out. "This is your suitcase, and you have mine. So if you don't mind...."

"Show the young lady in, Michael," the man in the wheelchair said.

Kate stepped back. "I don't think—"

It was too late. The cowboy had her by the arm, and was ushering her into the living room. Next came the apology, and then the explanation. "I was just getting ready to take your suitcase to the hotel. I was going to do it earlier, but I overslept...." He nodded at the suitcase. "My travel alarm is in there."

He looked so sincere, and so sorry, that Kate felt her anger drain away. "Ah, um, well, I guess you've been inconvenienced too."

Angelo spoke up. "Life is full of inconveniences. I remember a time when we went to Topeka, and our luggage ended up in Miami."

The man had fat cheeks, dark, snapping eyes, and a large belly. He also had a very large bandage on his head. Was this Michael Gordon's ill friend?

The cowboy said, "Excuse my manners. Angelo, this pretty lady with the golden-red hair and green eyes is Katherine—Katherine Devlin. Miss Devlin, this is my good friend, Angelo Bonini, and his daughter, Trina."

Angelo gave her a brilliant smile. "You must've met my wife downstairs. Maria is the light of my life. Wonderful wife, wonderful mother, wonderful cook."

Kate had a brief flash of déjà vu—Michael Downs and Peach Springs, Arizona—and felt her stomach knot. But she managed a nod. "Your wife said you don't have a private line up here, so if you'll give me my suitcase, I'll go downstairs and call a cab."

Michael pointed behind her. "Your suitcase is right there by the door. You look a little out of breath, Katie lady. Sit down and relax. I'll take care of the cab."

He was gone before Kate could stop him.

"Would you like some coffee or tea, Miss Devlin?" Trina was asking.

"No, thank you," Kate replied, sitting down in the nearest chair. Trina was smiling at her, and Kate found herself smiling in return. She also looked around the comfortable, homey living room for the first time. Dark green overstuffed furniture, doilies on the polished tables, and photographs of smiling faces everywhere. The large window, framed with lacy white curtains, overlooked the street, and somewhere in the background, between the sounds of traffic and honking horns, she could hear the tick-tock of a grandfather clock.

Trying not to fidget, Kate said, "Is this your first baby, Trina?"

Trina's pretty mouth dimpled at the corners. "Yes, it is. My husband is in the Air Force, but he gets to come home on leave when I have the baby. We're lucky. He's stationed at Beal Air Force Base, so he's only a few hours away."

"You're very lucky indeed," Kate said, feeling a tug of envy at the love she could see in the young woman's eyes.

"Do you have children?" Angelo Bonini asked.

Kate shook her head. "No...." No, I'm not married."

Angelo nodded and beamed.

A few minutes later, the cowboy

walked in carrying a white paper bag, and announced casually, "Change of plans. No point spending money on a cab. I'll borrow Angelo's car and take you to the hotel."

Ready to protest, Kate bit back her words. Cab fare was expensive, she was on a limited budget, and this hadn't been Michael Gordon's fault after all. "Okay," she said finally, "but if you don't mind, I'd like to get started now."

"Not yet." Michael opened the white bag and pulled out a sweet roll. "I haven't had breakfast, and these beauties are fresh out of the oven. Coffee or tea?"

Feeling a bit rankled, Kate said, "Coffee," and followed Trina and Michael into the bright yellow-and-white kitchen. Angelo rolled along behind them in his wheelchair, and positioned himself at the head of the oversized hardwood table.

Michael poured coffee into four flowered earthenware mugs while Trina put the rolls onto a large matching plate. They looked wonderful, and smelled heavenly. For the first time since her wake-up call, Kate realized how hungry she was.

Michael gave her a fetching smile. "Hope you're not on a diet. That's a nasty word around here."

Kate pulled her sweater closer around her, and shook her head. "I usually have the opposite problem. When I was home, my mother was forever feeding me fattening foods to put 'meat on my bones.' "

Michael's cornflower-blue eyes were sweeping over her again, but he didn't comment.

Angelo chuckled. "When we bought this place, we were about as trim as two people could get. Well, at least for a couple of Italians with normal appetites who lived above a deli. Then Maria got pregnant with Trina and put on some weight, and we added the bakery. That was our downfall."

Trina giggled. "I've always been on the plump side, but now…." She patted her belly. "The doctor says I'll probably have a nine-pound baby."

As the minutes ticked off and the amicable chatter continued, Kate could think of a lot of questions she would like to have asked, mostly pertaining to Michael Gordon, whose blue eyes kept meeting hers in teasing fire. But it was getting late, and before she knew it, Day Two of her vacation would be gone.

She made another mental journal entry:

> *I don't think he's Jack the Ripper, so I don't think he's dangerous* that *way, but he has a way of looking at me that turns my insides to mush. His eyes seem to go right through me.* Not *a good sign! I hate feeling vulnerable. I also have the feeling he finds this whole thing amusing, and I haven't changed my opinion of him. He's still cocky and arrogant! Above all, he's still a cowboy, and his name is Michael!*

Kate thought about the dream she'd had the night before, flushed, and looked at her watch. "Thank you all for the coffee and rolls, but it's getting late. I have an early dinner reservation—engagement—at the Tonga Room, Mr. Gordon, and I don't want to be late."

"It's Michael, Katie lady, and it's no problem. The car is parked in the alley. I'll bring it around."

Kate grimaced at the use of his nickname for her, but she managed to wish Trina good luck, thank Angelo Bonini for his hospitality, and say the appropriate things to his wife downstairs too, whose black eyes sparkled with something Kate suspected was close to eager anticipation. Matchmaking was clearly on the woman's mind.

Michael had taken the suitcase with him when he went to get the car, so Kate stuffed her hands into her sweater pockets and waited at the curb. When he finally pulled up in a rickety, smoking Chevy, she climbed in and closed her eyes. Without a doubt, she should have called a cab!

She continued her mental journal entry:

I'm delighted to have my suitcase back, and I'm grateful for Michael

Gordon's assistance, but I really should have insisted on calling a cab. Sunlight is spilling through the window, emphasizing the deep sheen of his skin, and the muscles in his arms, and….

"Why did you tell me your name was Devlin?" Michael asked suddenly.

Kate groaned. Of course he would have seen her name on the suitcase. "Devlin is my mother's maiden name. I use it occasionally."

"Not *your* maiden name?"

"No, I'm not married."

"And you prefer that name to your own?"

"When I'm traveling, yes. It's safer."

"Aha, so I guess you must travel a lot?"

"Every chance I get."

"That must be pretty uncomfortable for you. I mean, you admitted you aren't a good flyer."

More uncomfortable with the questions, and with the man who was sitting beside her, Kate snapped, "There are other ways to travel, you know. Like by car, bus, or train." She bit at her bottom lip. "I'm sorry, that was uncalled for. This just hasn't been a very good start to my vacation, that's all, and I guess I'm a little edgy."

She was suddenly aware that she was seeing things she hadn't seen during the cab ride to North Beach, and that they were very close to the bay. Kate leaned forward and asked, "Is this the way to the hotel?"

Michael gave her a mischievous grin. "I'm taking the scenic route, which is actually a shortcut. Roll down your window, and you can smell the salt air and the fresh crab."

At that same moment, Kate saw the sign that read *Fisherman's Wharf,* and couldn't hold back the excitement.

"It's quite a sight, isn't it?" Michael said gently. "Fishing boats bobbing in the water alongside the Wharf below Restaurant Row, crab vendors calling their wares, steam billowing out of the cauldrons, the flavors of shrimp, cracked crab, San Francisco sourdough bread, abalone, and cioppino, and the smell of the sea. There is no other place like it in the world."

"It's breathtaking," Kate said. "I had no idea it was so big.... Um, I've only seen it at night, and everything looks smaller at night...." She looked away and flushed. What on earth was wrong with her? Why couldn't she admit to this man, this cowboy, that she'd never been to San Francisco? That she had never been anywhere but Peach Springs, Arizona, and L.A., that she had gone into debt to take this one-week fantasy vacation, and that she was no more than a simple country girl with a big dream? Surely a man like Michael Gordon, who seemed perfectly comfortable driving around in a chuggedy car, whistled through his teeth at hotel doormen, and thought nothing about wearing blue jeans with holes in the knees, would understand. And therein, she decided, lay the problem. Of course he would understand. More than likely, he would even consider them kindred soul mates, use that knowledge to his advantage, and before she knew it, she would be shearing sheep in Blue Sky, Montana.

"Well, I agree it looks smaller at night," Michael was saying, "and it's definitely a lot more impressive with all the lights, but I happen to appreciate seeing the bay, and the green, rolling hills of Marin County in the background."

They'd driven beyond Fisherman's Wharf now, and for the life of her, Kate couldn't understand how this could be a shortcut to Nob Hill. And then suddenly, he was turning onto Hyde Street, and they seemed to be climbing for the sky. The street was incredibly steep, and Kate closed her eyes and hung on as the Chevy groaned and creaked with the effort. And she kept them closed until Michael reached California Street and said, "You can open your eyes now, Katie lady. We're only one block from the hotel."

Kate took a deep breath and unclenched her hands, but before she could tell him to let her out at the corner, he'd pulled into the circular driveway under the canopy, parked the relic of a car amid all the luxury vehicles and limos, and was hauling her suitcase out of the back seat.

The doorman was trying very hard to look the other way, and Kate ground out, “I’ll take it from here, Michael. Thanks for the ride.”

He gave her a gallant bow and a dimpled grin. “My pleasure. By the way, you might consider wearing the green silk tonight. It’s the color of your eyes, and it will knock your date on his ear.”

Dumbstruck, Kate could only stare after him as Michael tooted the horn and drove off, surrounded by a cloud of exhaust fumes and smoke.

Chapter Four

Michael had gone home after all, to put on his one good suit and pick up his car, and it had been a race with the clock. After dropping Kate off at the hotel, Michael returned to the deli with his head in a whirl. And yes, filled with golden-red hair and green eyes, the sweet scent of her, and the knowledge that Katherine Ann Callahan had been lying to him through her teeth. And after he'd paced the floor with plodding footsteps, grumbling and snapping every foot of the way, it had been Angelo who had finally put it into perspective. "Call the hotel, Michael. I know you want to join Katherine for dinner, but you had better make sure she is dining alone. You must also find out the time. The restaurant manager is a good friend of yours. Surely he will be able to help you."

"Tell me I'm crazy," Michael pleaded.

"I don't think you are crazy, my friend. I think you are falling in love."

Michael shook his head vigorously. "You can't fall in love in a matter of hours, Angelo."

"Who says? The first time I saw Maria, she was walking along Market Street. She was in the middle of the block, and by the time she reached the corner, I was in love. We were married two months later."

Trina was taking a nap, and Maria was downstairs in the deli, and Michael was more than grateful the women weren't there to hear him say, "I'm convinced she isn't rolling in money like she'd like me to believe, and I'd bet the bank this is her first trip to San Francisco, but what if she actually has a dinner date?"

Angelo replied, "You won't know until you make that call, Michael."

"What if I get to the restaurant, and she tells me to get lost?"

"Then I would suggest you get lost, and take comfort in the knowledge that it wasn't meant to be."

"But what if it wasn't meant to be, and I'm only chasing a dream?"

Angelo had said, "No man can predict the future, my friend. And what is life all about if it isn't to take chances?"

Michael had promptly gone downstairs to call the hotel, and it hadn't taken long to get the information he wanted. Katherine Callahan had a dinner reservation for six o'clock. Party of one, which meant she would be given a table for two because there was no such thing as a table for one in the Tonga Room. He'd requested two more favors—that she be given a table overlooking the pool, and that the tropical storm, which occurred every hour, begin at seven o'clock instead of nine. He'd braced himself then for Maria's reaction after he hung up the phone, but Maria hadn't told him he was crazy either, or any of those things he'd expected her to say. She'd given him a hug of encouragement, suggested he go home and put on his suit, and had promptly called him a cab.

Now it was six-fifteen and he was in the Tonga Room, standing behind a tangle of tropical foliage between the bar and the dining area, where he had a clear view of Katherine Callahan. His heart twisted at the sight of her. She looked so lost and alone he could hardly stand it. And she was wearing the green dress. Now all he had to do was get up the nerve to approach her table.

"Hey, Michael, how's it going?"

Michael turned around, and smiled. It was Grant Miller, head of Pediatrics at the hospital. He was a tall, thin man with a happy face, but at the moment he wasn't smiling. "Hello, Grant. Fancy meeting you here."

Grant's frown deepened. "I think that's my line. I thought you were supposed to be on your way to Blue Sky, Montana for a few weeks of R and R."

"Change of plans. Angelo had a dizzy

spell, and Maria called me while I was in L.A. I caught the next flight up, because I didn't want to take any chances. Fortunately, it wasn't anything serious. He's a determined man, and stubborn, and I think he was simply trying to do a little too much, too soon."

"Uh-huh. Well, then, maybe you can you tell me why you're wearing a suit, and why you're hiding behind a palm tree? Are you in trouble? FBI, Mafia, CIA, Internal Revenue, maybe the WSB?"

"The what?"

"Ha-ha, just a joke. That's the World Security Bureau—fictitious organization on a daytime soap. It's Winnie's favorite show."

Michael took a deep breath. "You see the redhead sitting at the table beside the pool? No, on the far side. The lady in the green dress."

"Well, how could I have missed *her?"*

"Yeah, well, don't let your wife hear you say that. I met her on the flight from L.A. She thinks I'm a sheep rancher from

Montana. Don't ask me to explain. I don't have the time."

Grant Miller finally grinned, and it landed from ear to ear. "Aha. Well, I wouldn't dream of asking you to explain, but if you'll let me make an observation, yeah, I'd say you're in trouble. Major big-time."

Kate didn't have a drink in front of her, and didn't look like she was interested in ordering one, or dinner. At the moment, she was speaking to a waiter, and shaking her head. Either she wasn't ready to order, or she wasn't going to stay. Michael said quickly, "If you were going to approach that lady, how would you go about it?"

Grant chuckled. "If she thinks you're a sheep rancher from Montana, I'd say you're off to a rocky start. For one thing, you shouldn't be wearing a suit."

"You think they'd let me in here wearing jeans and cowboy boots?"

"No, but you could've compromised, like you usually do. Slacks, cowboy boots, and a sport coat. Ties aren't required."

"My sport coat is in the cleaners."

"Well, if you want to get Winnie's advice, she's waiting for me in the bar."

Michael rolled his eyes. "I want *your* advice, Grant."

Grant shrugged. "You know how long it's been since I picked up a pretty lady?"

"This isn't a pickup. We've already met."

"Then go up to her table, kiss her hand, and tell her you want to buy her a drink. On second thought, maybe you should go out to the gift shop and buy her a flower or something. I don't think they close until eight."

Michael sighed. "Or something."

Grant patted Michael on the shoulder. "She means a lot to you, huh?"

"I met her just a little over twenty-four hours ago, Grant, and I don't know what I feel. I guess that's why I'm here. And maybe because I've decided to play her game. Don't ask me to explain that one either."

Grant smiled. "Wouldn't touch it on a bet. So, are you going to Blue Sky?"

"Maybe.... It depends."

"Well, if you want to talk, you've got

my number. Gotta go. Winnie is waiting."

In the length of time it had taken to have that conversation with Grant and make his way to her table, Michael had decided to use the casual approach, which didn't include buying Kate flowers or kissing her hand. It would be a lot easier that way, if he was in for a rejection. For sure, he wouldn't feel like such a jerk.

Michael took a deep breath and sat down across from her. "Small world," he said casually, but it was hardly the way he felt. He'd pictured her in the sea-green dress, but nothing could have prepared him for the real thing. Although the neckline was demure and the sleeves long, the silk fabric clung to every curve, and she had done something different with her hair.... Was he mistaken? Had her eyes suddenly come alive with dancing lights at the sight of him?

"H-hello, Michael," she said a little hesitantly. "I didn't expect to see you here."

"I didn't expect to be here. Some

friends called at the last minute, and we decided to meet here for a drink."

"Friends who knew you'd be at the deli?"

Michael nodded, and hoped that the flush he felt sweep his cheeks wasn't too obvious. Of course, the lighting, provided by tiki torches and candles, was pretty dim, and….

"So where are your friends?"

"In the bar. I had a drink with them, and now they are waiting for a table for Dinner…." For Pete's sake, she wasn't going to ask to meet them, was she?

"You're not going to join them for dinner?"

"No…."

Fish or cut bait, he was thinking, when she said, "You look uncomfortable in a suit."

"I *am* uncomfortable," he replied, "but this isn't exactly the place for cowboy boots and a Stetson."

Kate looked around, and her expression could only be called wistful, maybe even dreamy. "I had no idea it would be like this. I feel like I'm in a tropical paradise, with all the foliage, rattan furniture, the soft Hawaiian music, and the flickering lights reflecting across the pool."

"Didn't your date prepare you? It's a tropical paradise. And wait until you see the 'pool spectacular.' Once every hour over the pool, the heavens open up in an incredible display of thunder, lightning, and rain. It's all done with overhead pipes, lights, and sound, of course, but you'll swear you're in the middle of a tropical typhoon."

"I thought that didn't start until nine."

"Umm, well, they are going to start earlier tonight. Around seven, I think."

Kate's eyes lowered. "I don't have a date, Michael. I've never believed that having a dinner partner is a prerequisite for eating in a nice restaurant and, after all, I *am* a guest in the hotel. It's not like I'm roaming the streets at night or anything."

Michael tried to read the expression in her eyes, and couldn't. Nor could he discern the tone in her voice when she said, "You know, I was really angry with you after you dropped me off at the hotel. You mentioned this dress, which meant you'd looked in my suitcase, but then I looked in yours too, and that made us even. The only thing is, I was looking for a way to find you. I remembered you telling the cabbie you were going to a deli in North Beach and giving him the address, but I couldn't remember the name or the address. But you knew I was staying at the Fairmont."

"Meaning, there was no logical reason why I had to go into your suitcase? You wouldn't believe me if I told you."

"Try me."

Michael cleared his throat. "I remembered my sister telling me one time that if any of her luggage ever went astray, it had better not be the suitcase containing her nightclothes, makeup, and unmentionables. It was late when I got around to opening your suitcase, and when I found only clothing, well, I thought the exchange could wait until morning."

She looked like she understood, but then she was nodding toward the bar.

"There is a tall man waving at me, or maybe he's trying to get your attention."

Michael turned around, and gave Kate a reluctant shrug. "That's my friend. I'd better see what he wants."

Kate watched Michael hurry off toward his friend, and desperately tried to compose herself. When Michael had slipped into the chair across from her, as casually as he'd slipped into the seat beside her on the plane, she had been completely unprepared for her reaction. Her response to seeing him again had left her a little breathless, and definitely weak in the knees. She had tried to tell herself it was because he was wearing a light tan suit, and a very attractive silk tie, and that she could almost believe he wasn't a cowboy. But that hadn't been it. It had been the man himself, who in a matter of only a few hours had managed to work his way into her heart. She'd worn the green dress because he'd asked her to, even though she knew she'd never see him again, and yet she knew the minute she entered the restaurant, dining alone in a romantic setting like this would be a mistake. That was why she hadn't ordered a drink, or dinner, and just before his unexpected appearance, she'd been seriously considering going up to her room.

And now?

Michael was making his way back to the table, and gave her an apologetic smile. "Sorry for the interruption. Where were we? Oh, yes. I think I was trying to explain to you why I opened your suitcase."

"And I accept your explanation. Your friend looks very distinguished."

"He's a doctor."

"What did he want?"

"He wanted me to join him for dinner.

I said I had other plans.... Unless you'd rather be alone."

Aware that her leg had brushed his under the table, Kate swallowed deeply. "N-no, I'd appreciate the company."

At that moment, a waiter approached their table, and Michael took charge. "We'll have the deluxe dinner for two," he said easily, "and bring us two Tonga Room specials, but go easy on the rum."

After the waiter had gone, Michael explained, "The deluxe dinner will give us a sampling of all their specialties."

"It sounds like you've been here before," Kate said.

"I've been here a few times…."

"You mentioned a sister. Does she live in San Francisco?"

"No, she lives near Salinas. She and her husband own an artichoke farm. She's my only sibling."

Kate shook her head to clear it, and to remind herself that the man sitting across from her in the suit was a sheep rancher. "Ranching and farming must run in your family, but how did you get into sheep ranching in particular?"

Something unreadable flickered in his eyes again. It was the second time she'd seen that expression. The first time had been in the cab, driving into the city from the airport.

"My mother lives in Blue Sky," he said finally. "I was there visiting, and the opportunity presented itself. I got a good deal."

"And your father?"

"My father died when I was little. He had an incurable disease, and I remember feeling so angry that there wasn't a cure. I guess that's why I—" He broke off, and managed a smile. "Here comes the cocktail waitress with our drinks. Don't let the mugs throw you. They are supposed to look like a volcano."

Kate smiled, and took a sip. "Well, they look like volcanos, and the concoction tastes wonderful.

"How long have you known the Boninis?"

"Forever. Or it seems that way. Angelo's brother is married to my ex-fiancée's sister."

Kate wasn't exactly surprised he'd been engaged, though he truly didn't look like the marrying type. But then Michael Downs hadn't looked the type either, and he hadn't been. She watched the downward curve of his mouth. Okay, his ex-fiancee was a sore subject, so she tried something else. "You mentioned your friend when we were on the plane. You said he was ill, and that was why you were making the detour to San Francisco. I assume that friend is Angelo?"

"That's right. He had a tumor removed a couple of months ago, and it's been a slow recovery."

"Malignant?"

"No, thank goodness."

"Trina said her husband is in the Air Force, and that he'll be coming home on leave when she has the baby."

Michael brightened. "She's a good kid. She'll make a great mother. What about you, Katie lady? Do you have a job in L.A.?"

Kate had this all planned, should the occasion arise. She had made up her mind before she left L.A. that she was going to be *somebody* during her one wonderful week in San Francisco, should anybody ask. And several glamorous occupations were on her list, beginning with an actress. Maybe the stage. She had thought of it as a modern-day Cinderella story. *Her* Cinderella story. But for some reason, she couldn't bring herself to go that far. "I-I work for *Ms. California.* It's a women's magazine."

"I've heard of it," he said. "It's big-time. What do you do?"

Publisher, executive editor, senior editor.... The choice was hers, but she couldn't go that far either. "I'm an editor."

Michael raised a brow. "I'm surprised. I thought you might be an actress or a model."

Flattered, though she wasn't sure why, because the way he'd said it didn't sound flattering at all, Kate said, "I thought about doing something like that when I arrived in California, but I didn't feel like starving for years. Tinseltown is full of beautiful women."

His blue eyes met hers. "You wouldn't have starved, Katie lady. Hollywood is always in the market for beautiful, sexy women."

Another compliment, but it sounded as though he meant this one.

"So, where are you from originally?" Michael was asking.

"Portland, Oregon," she said quickly. She almost told him the truth, but because he was from Blue Sky, Montana, if he knew she was from a place called Peach Springs, Arizona, where cattle ranching was a way of life, he might get the idea they had a lot in common, when they didn't even come close.

"Siblings?" he was asking.

"One sister."

"So, we do have something in common. Parents?"

"Yes…."

"And do they live in Portland?"

"Yes…." Kate sighed with relief when the waiter brought their food, for it was much easier to concentrate on the scrumptious meal than to answer Michael's questions. And what a meal it was—paper-wrapped chicken, sweet-and-sour pork, moo-shu chicken, bowls of rice, fried rice and soft noodles, and every sauce imaginable.

Michael raised his mug. "To us, Katie lady."

They touched glasses, and their eyes met over the flickering candlelight. Michael was smiling, and it was a smile that reached all the way to her heart.

They ate in silence, but there was an

awareness between them, and they both knew it. And later, under a canopy of thunder and lightning, while the rain pelted the pool and the mist of it all surrounded them, Michael looked deeply into Kate's eyes and said, "I'm going to be in town at least one more day, and I was wondering if maybe you'd let me show you around tomorrow. Oh, I know you've been here before, and I know you plan to do quite a lot of shopping, but I'd like to make up for all your lost time. I was the one who mixed up the suitcases, after all."

No! Yes! I can't! I don't dare! Words spoken silently, while Kate fought with her emotions. Could she survive a whole day with the handsome cowboy? Could she survive spending a day without him? She took a deep, ragged breath. Now more than ever, it was important for her to keep up her facade—for herself as well as for Michael. In a few days he would be going to Montana, and she would be heading home. And that would simply be the end of it.

Choosing her words carefully, she said,

"I suppose it might be fun to see San Francisco through your eyes, Michael."

He leaned back in his chair and regarded her intently. "You mean, through the eyes of a sheep rancher?"

"Well, yes. I'm sure you must see things differently than I do."

He didn't look offended. Only amused. "Then you'll leave the plans up to me?"

Kate nodded and sighed, wondering what she had gotten herself into. No doubt they'd be taking Angelo's chuggedy Chevy, and that thought alone made her a little woozy.

"Michael! Well, hello! I ran into Grant, and he said you were here. Well, you can imagine how surprised I was. I'd heard you were in Blue Sky on that awful ranch."

Kate blinked, and looked up at the tall, willowy blond in the little black dress that plunged here and there, and showed a good deal of her long, shapely legs.

Michael gritted his teeth and cleared his throat. "Monica."

"Well, is that the best you can do?" Monica's eyes were on Kate, and her smile was cunning. *"I'm* doing terrific, thank you very much."

He cleared his throat again. "This is Kate Callahan. She's up from L.A.... Um, Kate, this is Monica Lang."

The woman nodded at Kate. "Hello, Kate Callahan. If I had the time, I'd ask you how you managed to get this cowboy into a suit. Not that he doesn't look gorgeous. When we were engaged, he insisted on looking like a bum, and nothing I could do or say would change him. Are you going to be in San Fran long?"

"She's going to be in the city a few more days," Michael snapped.

"And I suppose you're going to show her the sights? Well, don't forget to take her to Alioto's on the Wharf." She batted her long eyelashes at Kate. "It's a wonderful restaurant, and you haven't lived until you taste their stuffed shrimp. It was always Michael's favorite. Well, ta-ta, you two. My date is waiting."

More than baffled by the whole incident, Kate watched the woman walk away, and tried to sort it out. When Michael had said he'd been engaged, she'd pictured a pretty country girl. Maybe a local in Blue Sky, Montana. *Not* somebody like the glamorous, sophisticated, and very chic Monica Lang.

Michael said quickly, "How about some dessert? The melon sherbet is great, and the fortune cookies are made fresh every day."

Kate's head began to pound. "I don't think so, Michael. It's been a exhausting day, and I'd like to turn in early."

She reached into her purse to pay for her share of the meal, but Michael stopped her. "Dinner is on me, Katie lady. What time shall I pick you up tomorrow?"

Kate shrugged. "As a rule, I get up early…."

"Then let's make it around eight. I'll take you to breakfast, and we can go from there."

Kate thanked Michael for dinner, declined his offer to see her to her room, and hurried out of the restaurant before she broke out in tears and made a complete fool of herself. And even worse was realizing how much it mattered.

* * *

"You want to talk about it?" Angelo asked Michael later that evening. Michael was going to go home after he left the hotel, but he didn't want to be alone. Didn't want to call Grant either, or any of his friends, so he headed for the deli, and hoped Angelo would understand and offer some advice.

"That's why I'm here," Michael said, pouring coffee into a mug. He sat down at the kitchen table and sighed. "It ended up a disaster, Angelo. Everything was fine until Monica showed up."

"Whoa. That must have been awkward."

"It was. Kate knew I was engaged at one time, but I don't think she was prepared to meet the woman, no more than I was prepared to see her. And like always, it was worse than having a tooth pulled."

"Monica's claws were out, huh?"

"And then some. About the only good thing that came out of it was when I realized how wrong I'd been in the beginning, when I thought Kate and Monica were alike. Before I realized that she's been playing this little identity game. Seeing them together like that opened my eyes. Monica at her best couldn't be Kate at her worst. Now all I have to do is get Kate to open up, and tell me why she's been lying to me, and then maybe we can work it out. I'm picking her up in the morning, and we plan to spend the day sightseeing. She'll have ample opportunity, and I'll give her all the time she needs."

"And if she doesn't?"

"I have the feeling she will. I think she wanted to tell me tonight."

"And what about you, my friend? Are you going to tell her the truth?"

Michael sighed. "I'm going to tell her. I don't know how or when, but if this relationship is to have any chance at all, honesty has to come first. After that, we'll just have to see what happens. And think about it, Angelo. How angry can she get? She hasn't been honest with me either."

Angelo reached across the table and patted Michael's hand. "Sounds to me like tomorrow is going to be a day filled with discovery and revelations. I wish you well, Michael. I know Katherine means a great deal to you, but take my advice and go slowly. Find out her side of it first, and act accordingly, because I have the feeling it's a lot more complicated than it looks."

Michael shook his head. "I get that feeling too. So, what do I do? Do I wear my western apparel and rent a car? Take your Chevy? Try to look like a doctor, and hope she guesses I'm not who I claim to be either?"

"You go as Michael Gordon," Angelo said. "You drive your own car, and you dress as you normally would for a day-long sightseeing date with a beautiful woman. If you are willing to accept the *real* Katherine Callahan, no matter who she is, then she will have to be willing to accept you, and that includes taking the good with the bad."

Michael gave Angelo a feeble smile. "You make it sound like she's going to be the real loser here."

"Nobody will be the loser if your hearts beat together. Love has a way of working through all of that. It's late. Maybe you should spend the night."

Michael shook his head. "I'm going home, Angelo. I have the feeling I'm going to spend half the night pacing the floor, and the rest of the night talking to myself. But I'll call you tomorrow. Promise."

"I'll hold you to that promise, and remember, our prayers will be with you. You are a good man, and deserve the rich rewards of love and happiness, the kind of love and happiness my Maria has brought into my life."

Michael wasn't sure he deserved all that praise, but he left the deli with his footsteps much lighter than when he'd arrived, and, for the first time, he felt a glimmer of hope.

Chapter Five

I've never thought of myself as a weepy female, yet last night, I cried myself to sleep, because I finally had to admit I've fallen in love with Michael Gordon. Michael Gordon, the man, not the cowboy. The man who cared enough about his friend to delay his trip to Blue Sky, Montana. The man who knew I was going to have dinner in the Tonga Room last night, and who deliberately arranged to be there, concocting a story about a last-minute invitation to meet his friends for a drink. His story was so thin, I could see right through it. I know I should feel flattered, but all I feel is an overwhelming sadness, because he felt that he had to go through all that just to be with me. Was the suit for my benefit? Has my distaste for his life-style been that obvious? A life-style that I now realize doesn't matter at all, because had Michael Downs been a caring and considerate kind of man, like Michael Gordon, I would have married him in a minute, and eagerly shared his dream.

I also know it's crazy. How can a person fall in love in a matter of a few hours? He hasn't even kissed me, or held my hand. And yet the emotions I feel, and yes, the passions, are there, churning around inside of me, and they can't be denied. They are also very, very frightening.

Last night would have been wonderful if Monica Lang hadn't popped up unexpectedly. And what a shock it was. It also opened my eyes. If Michael is attracted to me, it's because he thinks I'm chic and sophisticated too. It's my fault, because that's what I wanted him to think. It's what this little fantasy vacation was all about, and chic and sophisticated is obviously the type of woman he likes. Well, they say opposites attract, but the joke is on me, because I'm not *Monica Lang, and never will be. Nor would I want to be. I'm who I am, through and through, and now it's over before it ever really began.*

This was to be our last day together anyway, so it's probably for the best. I left a note for Michael at the front desk. Simply put: Sorry I can't join you today, Michael, but I've had to change my plans. I'm leaving for L.A. this afternoon. Thanks for everything, and have a safe trip to Blue Sky. Sincerely, Kate.

I know leaving him a note like that was pretty cowardly of me, whereas I could have easily called the deli, but I didn't want to talk to the Boninis, or Michael. Nor did I lie. My plans have changed. I'm taking an afternoon flight home, because the sooner

I can get back to the normalcy of everyday living, and reality, the better off I'll be. The hotel room is paid for until Saturday—paid for in advance because I wanted to make sure I had the money—but I'm not going to ask for a refund. All that would do is make me feel cheap, and I feel ghastly enough. Besides, none of this is the hotel's fault. I didn't come to San Francisco to fall in love....

Kate closed the journal and sighed. It was barely eight o'clock, and her flight didn't leave until four. She would have to leave for the airport around two. Six more hours that were going to seem like a lifetime.

"So, now what do I do?" Michael said, tossing the note on the kitchen table.

Angelo shook his head. "Did you try calling her room at the hotel?"

"I did, and she didn't answer. I had a bellboy go up, but she wasn't answering the door, either. She had the 'Do Not Disturb' sign on the door."

Trina helped herself to a slice of coffee cake, and her dark eyes danced. "You could kidnap her. Take her off somewhere romantic, and woo her with your charms."

"Right, and how do you propose I do that when she won't come out of her room, and probably won't until it's time to leave for the airport?"

"So, wait for her at the airport, and abduct her there," Trina said.

"Uh-huh, and end up in jail."

Trina giggled. "I'll bake you a cake with a file. Seriously, Michael, there has to be a way. Unless, of course, you are simply going to let your 'Katie lady' walk out of your life."

Michael rubbed his forehead with his fingers. "I think that's my biggest dilemma, trying to figure out why she wants to walk out. This is only the third day of her vacation, and for some reason, she's giving it all up. Am *I* that reason? Last night, she agreed to spend the day with me. So what happened between then and now?"

"Did you say anything to upset her?" Angelo asked.

"I've squeezed my brain thinking about that, and with the exception of Monica showing up, I thought the evening went very well."

Trina whistled. "Monica Lang? You didn't tell me about that."

"I told your father last night, so why bring it up again? Monica stopped by our table to say hello, and dig a couple of digs, but I don't see how that could have upset Kate."

"Did she act upset at the time?" Angelo asked.

"Maybe a little, but not because of the things Monica said. Monica was just being Monica, and we all know what that means."

"So then why was she upset?" Trina pressed.

"To tell you the truth, I don't know. After Monica left, everything changed. The light had gone out of Kate's eyes. I asked her if she wanted dessert. She said she didn't, that it had been an exhausting day, and she wanted to go to bed early.

I told her I'd pick her up at eight, and the evening came to an end."

Angelo asked, "Did you see her to her room?"

"No. I offered, but she said it wasn't necessary. That's when I got the feeling she was trying to get away from me, and the sooner, the better."

"Do you think she's really going back to L.A. this afternoon?" Angelo asked.

"My friend the hotel manager said that the hotel switchboard confirmed she placed a call to the airlines this morning, so I'd say that's a safe bet. She's running away. It's the only explanation."

"Maybe she's falling in love with you too," Trina said. "And that's what's frightening her off. Sometimes love can be pretty scary."

Michael frowned. "Who said I'm falling in love with her, Trina?"

Trina rolled her eyes. "Come on, Michael. Do I look like I just fell off a turnip truck? Besides, Papa told me."

Michael tossed up his hands. "Is nothing sacred?"

Trina tittered. "Not around here. Papa

told Mama too, and that's why she was singing all morning, until you walked in and told her what happened. Now she's sad. When I went downstairs to get the coffee cake, she was slamming things around and muttering."

"You got Katherine to share a cab with you on the way into the city," Angelo said thoughtfully. "Maybe you can do that again. You know, be waiting out front of the hotel this afternoon, and force it, if you have to. She'd have to listen to you, Michael, or jump out of the cab along the freeway."

Trina squared her shoulders. "Well, that's the best idea yet."

"It's a lousy idea," Michael muttered. "You don't know her like I do. She'd probably clamp her hands over her ears and refuse to listen."

Angelo said, "I don't think you know her at all, Michael, and that's the problem."

Trina was drawing patterns on the flowered tablecloth with the tines on her fork, and gave Michael a sly smile. "You know what I think? I think you should figure out a way to get Kate on board the Sea Nymph, and take her out in the middle of the bay and keep her there until you have everything settled between you. I doubt very seriously that she'd try to swim to shore, so she'd have to listen."

Michael sighed. "But don't you see? That's the problem. Listen to what? To me tell her that I've fallen in love with her, I can't live without her, and I want her to give up her career and move up here? And do I tell her all that before or after I tell her I'm not a sheep rancher, and that I've been playing a game too? Either way, she wouldn't believe me. And I wouldn't blame her. People don't fall in love overnight." He looked at Angelo and waved a hand. "I know, you fell in love with Maria in a lot less time than that, but I've always been a realist. Monica and I dated for almost a year before I asked her to marry me."

Angelo snorted, "And where did that get you? And you talk about being a realist? Is that why you've been pretending to be somebody you're not?"

Trina was grinning mischievously.

"I'll bet if you got all dressed up, met her in front of the hotel with a limo, a bouquet of flowers, and your dazzling smile, you could talk her into going to the Sea Nymph with you. Meanwhile, you'd have a few hours. You could get things ready on board, like fill the salon with flowers and the galley with food. After a romantic candlelight dinner, well, who knows what might happen."

Michael closed his eyes, trying to picture it. It was an exciting thought, and what did he have to lose? When he opened his eyes, Trina and Angelo were watching him intently. Finally, he nodded his head. "Okay, you win. I'll give it a try. Just don't leave town. You might have to pick up the pieces."

Trina squealed with delight, but Angelo, though pleased, put it into perspective again. "Just remember to go slowly, my friend. You have a lot to resolve, and prudence is right up there with honesty."

Michael arrived at the hotel in the limo fifteen minutes early. He'd found out Kate's flight number and departure time easily enough, and allowing the one hour before the flight required by the airlines, and the one hour it would take to get down the peninsula to the airport, he figured she would leave the hotel around two o'clock. He'd also made arrangements with the front desk to ignore her request if she asked for a cab. Now all he could do was wait, and pray.

He was wearing white ducks, a polo shirt, and deck shoes, and the flowers were three dozen red roses. The limo came equipped with a bar, and the champagne was on ice. He had champagne on ice on the Sea Nymph too, and two-inch steaks ready to broil. And he had taken Trina's advice and had filled the salon with flowers—spring flowers, of every color and description. And yes, he was going to go slowly. He was also going to do what Angelo had suggested last night, and get her to open up first. And maybe by that time he'd have the nerve to tell her the truth.

At exactly two o'clock, Kate walked out of the hotel, wearing green slacks and a sweater. It had been a warm spring day, but now the fog was rolling in. She hugged the sweater close to her body, and headed for the bank of taxicabs. The doorman was right behind her with her luggage, but Michael headed them off.

"Kate."

She looked at him and frowned.

He began again. "Kate, these are for you." He handed her the flowers, and flushed. "I have a limousine waiting…."

She buried her face in the roses, and tears filled her eyes. "Y-you want to take me to the airport in a limo?"

"Well…." If he told her the truth, would she refuse? One more lie, and what could it hurt now? "Well, if it's okay with you."

She glanced at the cabs, and bit at her bottom lip. "Well, I guess it would be okay. Probably a lot more comfortable. And you've gone to all this trouble…."

Michael didn't wait for her to reason it out any further. He took her by the arm and whisked her away to the limo before she could change her mind. Nor did he dare breathe until they were on their way. He doubted that he would have said anything either, if she hadn't looked out the window and said, "This isn't the way to the airport, Michael."

At that point, he poured two glasses of champagne and tried for a roguish grin. "We're taking the scenic tour by way of the marina. I have—A friend of mine has a boat berthed there, and I thought….

Well, I thought it would be the best place for us to talk."

"Michael, I don't think—"

"Don't think, Katie lady. Just relax, and enjoy."

"But my plane ticket…."

"Did the airlines already reschedule your flight?"

"Yes. My flight leaves at four."

"Then they can reschedule it again. Originally, you weren't planning to leave until Saturday."

"I-I might have to buy another ticket…."

"Let's worry about that later."

Kate looked at him and shook her head. "Why are you doing this, Michael?"

Michael took a deep breath. "Because I don't want you to leave, at least not yet, not this way. I have too many things I want to say. Go with this, Kate, please…."

She had the roses in her lap, and touched the petals. Finally, she said, "Do I have a choice?"

"You have a choice," Michael said gently. "If you really want to go to the airport, I'll tell the driver."

Kate's sigh was heartfelt. "I think you're crazy. I think *this* is crazy, and maybe I'm crazy too, but I'll go with you. Just don't ask me to reason why."

Michael relaxed. "Fair enough."

In truth, Michael thought it was more than fair, under the circumstances, and his heart filled with warmth. And maybe even love.

Chapter Six

The Sea Nymph was berthed in a slip along the wide, well-maintained dock, where boats of every description bobbed in the rolling water. No one seemed to be out and about, and Michael explained it was because the day had turned dark and dreary with the incoming fog. Kate knew nothing about boats, but this one was a beauty, reminiscent of the one she had always admired on the defunct TV show *Miami Vice,* belonging to Sonny and his pet alligator.

Michael produced a key and said, "The

owner is a doctor friend of mine, and gave me an extra key."

"The doctor who was in the Tonga Room last night?" Kate asked.

"No. The doctor who owns the Sea Nymph is a surgeon. He uses it on weekends, so the galley is always well stocked. She's a cruiser, and is equipped with a galley, salon, two staterooms, and a head with a shower. She's also hooked up to electricity and water, so we'll have all the comforts of home. I'd take her out for a run, but the fog is getting pretty thick."

Within seconds, they were inside the cozy, elegantly decorated salon, and out of the biting sea air.

Kate stood in the middle of the salon and looked around appreciatively at the rich, dark wood paneling, muted fabrics in shades of blue and green, and plush carpeting, and at all the flowers spilling over everywhere. White and yellow jonquils and tulips. Pink carnations and roses. "You must have been pretty sure I'd come," was all she said.

"I wasn't sure at all, but I was hoping." He moved to the portable bar and uncorked a bottle of champagne. "You look uncomfortable, Kate. Are you upset because I let the limousine go?"

"I'm not upset, exactly, but it makes me feel vulnerable, knowing I'm here with no way to leave."

"Leaving would be easy enough. There isn't a phone on board, but there is a pay phone near the boat shop, and another one out on Marina Boulevard, about a block down. I couldn't tie up the limo all afternoon, Kate. When it's time to leave, I'll call a cab."

Michael had carried a tote on board, along with Kate's luggage, and from the tote he produced two crystal glasses that had been wrapped in a towel. "When I was here earlier to get things ready, I noticed all the doctor had on board were plastic glasses."

Kate had barely touched the champagne in the limo, and she didn't want any now, but Michael looked so expectant, she couldn't refuse. No more than she could deny the awareness she felt. Michael was wearing white duck pants and a polo shirt, and she could smell the musky scent of him from across the room. And his cornflower eyes were on her, drinking in the sight of her, like he wanted to preserve every detail. Or was he wondering where his "Katie lady" was? The pants and sweater she was wearing were hardly glamorous, and she hadn't bothered to apply makeup. Hadn't done much with her hair either, except to pile it on her head. *What you see is what I am, Michael,* she said to herself.

She sat down in a blue club chair, and cleared her throat. "You said you wanted to talk…."

"Later, Kate. Right now I want you to relax."

She looked at the roses in her lap. "We'd better get these in water."

Michael took them from her, put them in the ice bucket in place of the champagne, and sat down across from her. "I guess you've figured out by now that I'm trying very hard to make an impression."

"Like you were trying to make an impression last night?"

Michael frowned. "I don't understand."

"You were wearing a suit, Michael,

and you admitted you were uncomfortable. I can only assume you wore the suit to impress me. Assuming, of course, I'm right, and your appearance at the Tonga Room wasn't a coincidence, and had nothing to do with meeting your friends for a drink. If you wanted to take me to dinner, why didn't you just say so?"

"You said you had an 'engagement' for dinner. That sounded like you had a date to me, and if you didn't, you wanted me to think you did. I had to be sure. And yes, I was uncomfortable. Suits aren't my style."

"I gathered that when Monica wanted to know what I'd done to get you into a suit. Meeting her like that was quite a shock. She wasn't what I expected for a—" She broke off, unable to go on.

The muscles worked along his jawline. "For a sheep rancher from Montana?"

"Well, yes, and it was just one more piece of the puzzle I couldn't put together. You looked so at home in the Tonga Room. You took charge and did the ordering, knew what fork to use, and— Well, your manners were impeccable.

You have a lot of important friends too, like doctors, and then with a woman like Monica on your arm, well, it's easy to see you've enjoyed having the best of both worlds."

"Both worlds?"

"Glitzy city life and sheep ranching."

"So, in your book, you think all ranchers are barbarians?"

Kate lifted her chin. "No, of course not. My—" She broke off again, struggling with her emotions. She was about to tell him her father was a rancher, but she couldn't bring herself to say the words. She took a deep breath. "Monica is a beautiful woman. How did you meet her?"

"I met her through some friends."

When it was obvious he wasn't going to go on, she said, "What does she do for a living?"

"She's a fashion model.... Look, I don't want to talk about Monica. I want to talk about you."

"I'm afraid you'd find it quite boring by comparison," Kate muttered, getting to her feet. "Which way to the rest room?"

"The head is aft. That's in the rear." Kate nodded, and hurried out of the salon.

It wasn't going well, and for the life of him, Michael couldn't figure out why. Unless it was Monica. Meeting the woman had obviously bothered Kate more than he realized, and now the tension was thicker than ever. He hadn't wanted that. Nor had he expected to see so much sadness in her eyes. She was like a little kid, standing in front of a candy store window without a penny in her pocket, and he didn't understand that either.

At that moment, his pager went off. He'd told the Boninis to page him if they needed him. He pulled the unit from his tote. It was the phone number for the deli, and he quickly scribbled Kate a note.

I have to make a quick phone call, Kate. I'll use the pay phone at the boat shop, so I shouldn't be long. Make yourself comfortable, and help yourself to the champagne.

By the time Kate returned to the salon, she knew she couldn't stay. This had been a mistake. She should never have agreed to come with him. Reality was in Los Angeles. Not here, with a perplexing sheep rancher from Montana, who obviously enjoyed mixing glitz and glamor with the life of a farmer.

Prepared to tell Michael to take her to the airport, or call her a cab, Kate was met with only silence, and the note on the chair where she had been sitting.

Kate read the note twice before she realized this was her chance. It wouldn't be easy, hauling her suitcases all the way out to the avenue, but she was determined. Michael said there was a pay phone a block away, and she could call a cab from there.

Not bothering to leave Michael a note, Kate carried her suitcases out to the deck and stood there for a moment, listening. The fog was thick, stealing across the water, reaching out to envelop everything in its path. But she welcomed it, because it would give her cover while she made her escape.

Kate waited a few more minutes, and then started down the gangplank. Halfway down, the toe of her shoe caught on a rough spot and sent her sprawling. She uttered a cry, tried to catch her balance, and fell headlong into the icy water between the boat and the dock. For an instant, she felt the pain in her head as she went under, and then knew only darkness.

The call to the Boninis was brief but worrisome. "I am so sorry to bother you, Michael," Maria said, "but Trina has been complaining of a backache the last few hours. Still, she says it is nothing, and won't let me call her doctor. She doesn't know about this call either, and it is times like this when I'm glad we don't have a private line upstairs."

"It's times like this when I wish you did, Maria. Does it appear to be the beginning of labor to you?"

"I don't know. When I had Trina, all

the pain was in front. But I remember when my sister had Tony. Her pain was in her back."

"Has she had any other discomfort?" Michael asked.

"No. Shall I call her doctor anyway?"

"I think that would be a very good idea. Things aren't going as well as I expected here, so it's possible I'll be leaving soon. I'll put Kate in a cab for the airport, and head your way."

Maria clucked her tongue. "Then you are on your boat?"

"Yes, we are. Look, I don't want to get into it now, okay?"

"It is not okay. Did you meet her with a limousine and give her flowers?"

"Yes, I did, but I don't think she was impressed. To tell you the truth, I don't even know why she agreed to come with me. Now she thinks I'm a playboy sheep rancher, who collects glamorous women as a hobby."

"Did she tell you that?"

"She didn't have to."

"Then you haven't told her the truth."

"No, and I'm not going to. Why confess

and bare my soul, when it will only fall on deaf ears?"

"I think you are making excuses, Michael. Tell Katherine you love her, and let that be your guide."

"You make it sound easy, and it isn't. I have to go. If there are any further developments with Trina before I can get there, page me again."

Michael hung up, and was on his way back to the boat, when he heard the scream and the splash. It was coming from the vicinity of the Sea Nymph, and there was no doubt in his mind that it was Kate!

With no time to think, or do anything but run, Michael covered the distance in a few seconds, but was met with only silence.

With his heart pounding up in his ears, and feeling overwhelming anguish, he was standing on the dock, trying to decide what to do, when he heard the tiny splash in the water between the dock and the boat. Silently giving a prayer of thanks for all those youthful summers he'd spent as a lifeguard, he held his breath and jumped in….

Kate woke up in bed in a stateroom on board the Sea Nymph, with Michael hovering over her. It took a moment for her head to clear enough for her to realize what had happened. She remembered the pain in her head and the cold, murky

Water…Had Michael saved her life?

She moved both feet and hands and found everything to be in working order, but what was wrong with her head? Something heavy, constricting….

When she reached up, Michael stopped her. "You have a nasty gash on your forehead, Kate. I've patched it up."

"Serious?" Kate asked in a whispery voice.

"No, or I'd have you in the hospital. It was enough to knock you silly though, so I don't want you up and around. At least not tonight. You might have a slight concussion."

"And you don't consider that serious enough to put me in the hospital?"

"Under normal circumstances, but….

Well, my sister had a concussion once, so I know all the signs."

Kate could see the concern in his eyes, and the tight lines around his mouth, and had to believe him. "You pulled me out of the water? Now I remember. The water was so cold.... I remember floundering, and then feeling somebody grab me...."

"I was on my way back to the boat when I heard you cry out, and then the splash. I couldn't imagine what had happened, Kate, and I nearly panicked."

"My—my suitcases...."

"I fished one of them out of the water. Your tote and the other suitcase were still on the gangplank. Fortunately, the suitcase that got dunked wasn't the one with all your good clothes. I've strung your undergarments and nightclothes over a line in the other stateroom. Not much chance of getting them dry in this weather, but it's better than leaving them in the suitcase." He gave her a level look. "Where were you going, Kate? Were you running out on me?"

Kate lowered her eyes. "I-I thought it was for the best. I should have let it end at the hotel. It was a mistake to come here When I read your note, I knew what I had to do. I was on my way to the pay phone on the avenue to call a cab. I started down the gangplank, and tripped and fell. I'm a good swimmer, but…."

"You probably hit your head on the gangplank, Kate. You could be the best swimmer in the world but it wouldn't have mattered. If I hadn't gone to make that call…."

At that moment, Kate realized Michael was wearing a robe. Well, of course. He'd gotten wet saving her. Her breath caught in her throat. Ever so slowly, she slipped a hand under the covers and along her body. No wet clothes. Something flannel, and warm….

Michael was saying, "I'll be in the galley, whipping up one of Maria's cure-all concoctions. Guaranteed to make you feel one-hundred-percent better. If you need another blanket or anything, let me know."

After he'd gone, Kate closed her eyes, mortified to think he'd undressed her. Then she reasoned that he'd had to. She was unconscious. He couldn't leave her shivering and miserable in wet clothing. But oh, the thoughts whirling around in her head! He had saved her life and she was grateful, but facing him now wasn't going to be easy.

He had her head wrapped in a towel, and she raised up to remove it. Not bad. No headache, though there was some discomfort at the site of the wound.

She was sitting on the edge of the bed, with a blanket wrapped around her, when Michael returned, carrying a glass full of amber-colored liquid.

"You shouldn't be up," he said matter-of-factly.

"I feel fine, honest," she replied, finding it more than difficult to look at him. Part of it was because he was wearing a blue robe the color of his eyes, and the rest of it was genuine embarrassment.

"Well, drink this, and let's see how you do."

"What is it?"

"Tea with a little honey and brandy. It's hot, so be careful."

It tasted wonderful, and Kate drained the glass.

He looked pleased, and even smiled as he rubbed a finger along her cheek. "I know you're trying to find the words to tell me off because I had to undress you, Kate, but I'm.... I closed my eyes, honest."

She took a deep breath. "Am I wearing your friend's pajamas?"

"And several large safety pins. It was the best I could do. Are you warm enough?"

Kate nodded and touched her damp hair. "I'd feel better if I could dry my hair. Does your friend have a hair dryer on board?"

Michael said, "I'll take a look."

A few minutes later, he returned carrying a hair dryer. He grinned and said, "I also found a brush. Don't worry. I washed it out."

When she reached for the hair dryer, Michael shook his head. "No, let me. There's an outlet behind the night table."

Kate turned so Michael was behind her, and closed her eyes. The warm air felt wonderful, and his strokes were gentle as he brushed out her hair. It was almost hypnotic, and Kate found herself leaning into him.

Michael turned off the hair dryer and groaned. When he wrapped his arms around her, he murmured, "I promised myself I wouldn't do this…."

"And I promised myself I wouldn't let you," Kate whispered, with her heart hammering in her ears. Warning bells were clanging too, but she was powerless to stop him, or the sweet kisses he rained over her neck and cheek. Finally, she turned her face for his kiss, and felt nearly faint as the soaring emotions coursed through her body. His lips were soft, as she knew they would be, and the kiss was tender, but oh, with the promise of much, much more.

Michael was the one to pull away. But not before she could see the open desire in his eyes.

"We'd better get your hair dry," he said shakily. "We don't want you catching a cold."

Colds start with a virus, she wanted to

tell him, but turned around again so he could finish drying her hair, even though she was more intent on the man than the appliance. His robe had opened to the waist, and Kate found her eyes riveted on his muscular, golden chest.

A few minutes later, Michael put the hair dryer aside, and took a deep breath. "I think you should rest now."

Kate took a deep breath too. She felt nearly out of control, and it was crazy. No, it was dangerous, because if this went too far, she wouldn't be able to escape….

He picked up the hair dryer absently, and she watched his hands as he turned the appliance over and over. He had long, slim fingers. She hadn't noticed before, but his nails were clean and well manicured. She thought it was strange, but then her musings were put on hold, because Michael had pulled her into his arms again, and was murmuring against her hair, "What are we going to do about this, Katie lady?"

Struggling to find the right words, and with her heart breaking, Kate finally said, "We're going to behave like adults, Michael, and walk away from it. You have your life and I have mine. I guess that's what I've been trying to tell you all along. Now, if you'll call a cab…."

Michael pulled away and scowled. "You received a nasty bump on the head, so you won't be going anywhere tonight."

Kate's response was instant. "Well, I'm not staying here!"

"Then as soon as you feel well enough, we'll take a cab to the deli. You can spend the night with the Boninis. I have to check on Trina anyway. That was the call I made. Trina is having some problems, and—"

Concerned quickly replaced anger. "The baby?"

"I'm not sure. Maria is going to call Trina's doctor. Meanwhile, I want you to get some rest."

Kate was about to protest, when she heard the beeping sound coming from the galley.

Michael frowned. "That's my pager. I told Maria to page me if there were any changes." He looked down at the robe. "I'll have to get dressed…." He fished around in one of the drawers and came up with jeans and a sweatshirt. "Try to relax, Kate. I shouldn't be gone long."

The minute Michael left the boat, Kate got to her feet. She felt light-headed and a little unsteady, but she was also determined to get dressed. Who knew what the rest of the day had in store, and she wasn't about to face it in a pair of men's flannel pajamas!

Michael was gone for fifteen minutes. When he returned, Kate was waiting for him in the galley, wearing a pair of tan pants and a sweater. She had water on for tea, and was prepared to retaliate if he decided to yell at her for being up.

But he didn't. He sat down at the table and sighed. "It was Maria. The doctor didn't seem too concerned. Said just to keep an eye on Trina, and keep him advised. Maria wanted to let me know so I wouldn't worry. I told Maria about what happened to you, and that you'd be spending the night with them."

"I don't know, Michael. I don't want to

put them out, and with all Trina's problems.... I think I'd rather go to the hotel.

I'm sure I could get another room. I have some credit coming, and—"

"I don't want you to be alone tonight, Kate, and that's that. And you won't be putting the Boninis out. They are looking forward to having you." He looked at his watch. "It's getting late. I have two steaks in the fridge...."

Kate shook her head. "I don't think I could eat something that heavy."

He studied her face. "Are you nauseated?"

"No, not really."

He opened a cupboard. "Well, how about some soup? Tomato, cream of chicken, or vegetable?"

"Tomato."

He put on an apron, oblivious to its frilliness, and opened the can. He looked so silly, and so wonderful, that Kate couldn't help but smile. "Is your doctor friend, who owns this boat, married?"

"No, why?"

"Well, you're wearing a feminine apron."

He looked down, like he was seeing it for the first time. "He's had his share of women friends. The apron probably belongs to one of them." He looked at her again. "Would you mind if I asked you a question?"

Kate shrugged.

"I hope that's a yes. I've had the feeling from the moment we met on the plane that you don't care much for cowboys. Or ranchers. Or western types in general. Is there a reason for that?"

"I was engaged to a cowboy," she said simply, "and it wasn't a pleasant experience. That's why I was so curt on the plane. You were obviously interested in me, and wanted to strike up a conversation, but.... Well, it isn't important now."

"I wasn't interested in you *that* way on the plane, Kate. I saw you were ill, and wanted to help, that's all."

Kate felt as though she'd been smacked in the face, but kept her composure. "That's right. You make a habit of helping damsels in distress. My mistake. Sorry."

“No need to be sorry,” he said glumly. “We all have our crosses to bear.”

It was a strange statement, and so was his expression. He looked so sad, it twisted her heart. Suddenly, surprisingly, Kate wanted to get Michael out of his gloomy mood. “Could a boat this size make it all the way to Hawaii?”

“I guess so. Sure, I don’t see why not. People have made it across the ocean in a lot less.”

“It sounds wonderful,” Kate said dreamily. “Nothing but water and sky. And you could use the sails when it’s windy, and the engine…. It does have an engine, doesn’t it?”

Michael finally smiled, though it didn't reach his eyes. “She has two inboard diesel engines. I suppose as long as you’re not prone to seasickness, it might be fun. A challenge. Have you ever been to Hawaii? I mean, in the conventional way.”

“No, I haven’t. I told you I’m no good at flying, and the thought of spending five hours in the air is frightening.”

“You’re safer up there than you are on the ground,” Michael said, placing a bowl of soup in front of her. "Eat it while it's hot, Kate."

Kate looked down at the creamy liquid, felt light-headed again, and this time she was nauseated. "I think I'd better lie down," she said quickly, struggling to get to her feet.

Michael helped her into the stateroom and into bed. He also gave her the devil for getting out of bed in the first place, and told her that unless she wanted to end up in the hospital, she'd better stay put.

And then he did a strange thing. He asked her to look at him while he stared deeply into her eyes. He also asked her to follow his finger with her eyes. After making a few satisfied grunts, he walked out of the room.

Left to puzzle over his behavior, Kate finally closed her eyes and dozed.

Awakened by a shake, Kate looked up into Michael's expressionless face. "You've been asleep a couple of hours," he said. "Feel better?"

She sat up and nodded. "Much better."

"Good, because I've called a cab. Think you can make it to the street?"

Kate nodded, and allowed Michael to help her to her feet. The rest was a blur as Michael hurried her off the boat.

They'd gone half the distance, when Kate stumbled. Before she could explain that she'd simply tripped over an uneven spot in the pathway, Michael put down her suitcases, explained he would come back for them as soon as she was settled in the cab, and swooped her up in his arms. Kate didn't protest. Sheep rancher or not, she felt safe in his strong arms, and snuggled close.

Chapter Seven

It was dark by the time they reached North Beach. As a precaution, Michael insisted on making two trips into the deli—one to escort Kate, and one with her luggage. But he didn't argue when she insisted she felt well enough to walk the distances unassisted. It wasn't altogether true, of course, because her legs still felt a little wobbly, but as much as she'd found his arms comforting before, she knew she would find no comfort in them now. From the moment they'd gotten into the cab, the change in Michael had been swift, and as puzzling as his behavior earlier. Gone was the concern and warmth he'd displayed before. It had been replaced with a curious kind of indifference, maybe even anger, that had left Kate huddled in the corner of the cab, feeling totally miserable. And even when he spoke to the cabbie, his words were clipped.

A security light was on in the store, and although it was after hours, the wonderful smells still lingered. Kate hadn't been able to eat the soup, and now she was hungry. But there was no way she was going to ask him to bring along a loaf of bread and a hunk of cheese, not even if she offered to pay for it.

Michael helped her up the stairs, saw to it she was in the living room, and then went back for her luggage.

Maria met her with a hug and ushered her into the kitchen, where Angelo was sitting at the table reading the paper and drinking a glass of milk.

Angelo gave her a broad smile. "Well, pretty lady. I understand you've had quite an experience. With all that's happened, I have the feeling Michael didn't get the chance to feed you. Sit down, and have some of Maria's homemade soup."

"I've kept it hot on the stove," Maria said. "You look chilled, and it will help warm you up."

Angelo pointed at the bandage on her forehead, and patted the bandage on his head. "We are twins. Only I think I would rather have a conk on the head. That wasn't meant to sound like you didn't have a bad fall, but if Michael thought it was serious, he'd have you in the hospital."

Kate sighed. "In the mood he's in, I'm surprised he didn't toss me overboard and feed me to the sharks. I know he's concerned about Trina.... How is she?"

Maria smiled. "She is doing better. The backache is gone. I think we were worrying needlessly, though as a precaution, I'm making her stay in bed. And she has an appointment with her doctor in the morning, so we will know more then."

A few minutes later, Michael deposited Kate's luggage in the little room off the kitchen and muttered, "I'm going to check on Trina."

"And then you will have a bowl of soup?" Maria asked brightly.

"I'm not hungry, Maria. I have some errands to run, and I'm not sure how long I'll be. I'll grab something to eat while I'm out."

Maria nodded. "Well, if you're not back by the time we go to bed, I'll have the couch in the living room made up. And I'll leave some soup on the stove, in the event you change your mind."

Aware that Michael was going to sleep on the couch so she could have the spare bedroom, Kate said, "I don't want to put you out, Michael. I'll sleep on the couch."

He didn't look at her, but snapped, "You'll sleep in the bedroom, Kate, and that's final."

After he'd gone to look in on Trina, Kate gave the Boninis a helpless shrug. "See what I mean? He's acting like this is all my fault, when it isn't! It isn't *my* fault he came to my assistance on the plane, or that he mixed up our suitcases, or that we ended up on that boat this afternoon. Well, I guess that part of it was my fault. I didn't have to go with him. If I hadn't, I'd be home by now, where things are sane and normal!"

Maria cleared her throat. "Why did you go with him, Katherine?"

"I've been asking myself the same question. I guess it was because he looked so hopeful, and he'd gone through so much trouble. He hired a limo, and bought me roses…." She looked away. "I left them on the boat. He was in such a hurry…" Her mind began to drift to another journal entry:

I was beginning to think the sheep rancher from Montana was a pretty nice guy, which just shows you how wrong you can be, and how easily you can get taken in. Caring one minute, a creep the next. Just like Michael Downs, whose idea of a gift was a pair of knee pads so I could wax the kitchen floor properly. I can't help but remember the time I sprained my ankle, and how angry he was. Like it was my fault I tripped over his boots. He was the one who left them in front of the door. Well, Michael Gordon doesn't have to worry. First thing tomorrow morning, I'm going home, and will try very hard to put this nightmare behind me.

"Michael has a lot on his mind," Angelo was saying. "And he can be difficult. But he is a good man."

Kate sniffed. "Well, I know all about difficult cowboys. I was engaged to one, and that was a nightmare too."

Maria placed a bowl of soup in front of Kate, along with a cup of coffee and chunks of Italian bread, and sat down at the table. "You were engaged to a cowboy?"

Kate caught the curious glance Maria exchanged with her husband, and nodded. "It's a long story, and I'd rather not go into it. But I will say this. His name was Michael too, and that alone should have given me fair warning.

"The soup tastes wonderful, Maria. I guess I was hungrier than I realized."

Maria beamed. "That is good! You are also exhausted, so after you eat, you will go to bed. Things will look better in the morning."

Kate was going to say she doubted it, but Michael had entered the kitchen. He briskly announced, "Trina seems to being doing just fine, so I'll head out now."

And just as briskly, he was gone.

Maria muttered something in Italian, but managed a smile. "I am sure you have your own nightclothes, but if not, you can borrow one of Trina's gowns. She wears mostly flannel, even in the summertime, because the nights in San Francisco can be cool."

Kate groaned. "In Michael's rush to leave the boat, I forgot my underwear and nightclothes. They got wet, and Michael had them hanging in one of the staterooms."

"Then Michael will just have to go to the boat in the morning," Angelo said stoutly. "And if they aren't dry, Maria can put them in the dryer."

Kate nodded, and gritted her teeth, wondering if she was ever going to get away from San Francisco.

* * *

Kate sat up in bed with a start. Disoriented at first, wondering if she'd had a bad dream, she heard the deep moans, and realized they were what had awakened her. They were the suffering, guttural sounds of a wounded animal. Or, she thought, quickly climbing out of bed, of a woman in hard labor.

Remembering the discomfort Trina had been in earlier, Kate hurried down the hall. Maria met her at the doorway to one of the bedrooms, and held up a hand. She looked tired and haggard, but there was a smile on her face. "It's the baby," she said. "The baby will be here soon, and then we can celebrate!"

Kate asked, "Then there wasn't time to get her to a hospital?"

Maria shook her head. "Trina wanted to have the baby at home, but there wouldn't have been time to get her to the hospital anyway. But it doesn't matter. She is in very good hands."

"Then her doctor is here?"

Maria's dark eyes twinkled. "Might not be such a good idea for you to go in, if you haven't had children, or seen a birthing. But maybe you might like to take a peek?"

Kate pushed toward the door. "I've helped deliver puppies, kittens, colts, and calves. How much different can it be?"

Maria smiled, and stepped aside.

Kate took three steps into the bedroom and froze. Michael was at the foot of the bed, and he was delivering Trina's baby!

"I need you now, Maria," he said. "Trina needs to hold your hand!"

Maria immediately rushed to her daughter's side and grasped a hand. She began cooing in Italian, and wiping the perspiration from Trina's brow.

Kate, who still wasn't getting the whole picture, moved like a zombie to the other side of the bed. She took Trina's left hand in her own, and chanced a glance at Michael. He looked calm and cool, and very much in charge.

He looked at her, and shrugged. "I had my reasons for not telling you."

Not telling me what? Kate wanted to scream. And then she had the whole picture. "You're a doctor?" she said, nearly strangling over her words.

Maria beamed. "He is the best doctor in San Francisco. He operated on my Angelo and saved his life."

Michael muttered, "We'll talk about it later." And then his total concentration was on Trina. "That's it, sweetheart. Take a nice cleansing breath after each contraction."

Trina looked up at Kate and managed a smile, and then her eyes squinted shut as her body was racked with pain.

"Did you alert the hospital and Trina's obstetrician?" Michael asked Maria.

"I did, and I told the doctor what you said."

"Yeah, well, I'd say the time is now. Trina, sweetheart, look at me."

Trina opened her eyes, and although they were filled with pain, they also held love and trust.

"Remember what I told you?"

She nodded. "You said you'd deliver my baby here if there wasn't time to get my doctor, but if you ran into trouble…." Her eyes opened wide. "Oh, no!"

"I don't think it's serious," Michael said quickly, "but it's my guess the baby is in a transverse position. You're going to need some help, sweetheart, and I simply don't have the equipment here. The hospital has been alerted, and so has your doctor. Maria is going downstairs now to call for an ambulance."

Trina clutched at Michael's hand. "Will you go with me?"

"Of course I will, and your mama will come too. Now let's get you ready for those good-looking medics in white."

"Is there something I can do to help?" Kate asked, trying to calm her racing heart.

Michael glanced at her. "Actually, there is. Angelo is in the kitchen, no doubt out of his mind with worry. Why don't you go give him some moral support? And while you're at it, you can remind him that now he has one more reason why he should get a phone line put in up here."

Kate nodded, and leaned over to kiss Trina's cheek. "Good luck, honey. I just know everything is going to be fine."

Trina managed a wan smile. “Me too, ’cause Michael will be there with me.”

Kate hurried out, but not before she saw the look of apprehension on Michael’s face, giving her the feeling that it was much more serious than he was letting on. Suddenly, nothing mattered but Trina and the baby, and she said a silent prayer.

Surprised to see Angelo out of the wheelchair, Kate walked into the kitchen, and admonished, “Michael wants you to stay in the wheelchair, Angelo.”

He was standing at the window, looking down at the avenue, and touched the bandage on his head. “I’m tired of the wheelchair, and I’m tired of this. I wear the bandage so I don’t have to look at the scar, and be reminded of that night I almost died, but what does it matter now? I know Maria is downstairs calling the ambulance, and I know that it’s serious. My Trina is having problems.”

Kate looked at the clock on the wall. It was four-thirty. It would be light soon, the beginning of a new day. "I know you haven't had much sleep, Angelo, so please sit down. Would you like me to fix you a cup of coffee? Maybe a cup of tea?"

"My stomach feels upset," he said, sitting down at the table. "The store will be closed today, and I'll be stuck up here worrying and waiting. Robert, Trina's husband, is on his way, but he will want to be with his wife at the hospital…."

Kate sat down across from him and took his hand. "You won't have to wait alone, Angelo. I'll be with you."

He gave her hand a pat. "You are a good person, Katherine. It's too bad our Michael is wearing blinders."

Aware that the door was open for all the questions she wanted to ask him, she began with, "Do you happen to know why Michael didn't tell me he's a doctor?"

Angelo sighed. "I know you are full of questions, as you have every right to be. But Michael will have to be the one who answers them."

And just as suddenly, the door was closed. "I'm not sure Michael will answer my questions," she said finally. "We've had a strange relationship at best."

"A relationship that has spanned what? Some thirty-six hours? That is hardly enough time to get acquainted under normal circumstances."

Kate was about to tell him she didn't think a lifetime would be enough time, when Tina let out a bloodcurdling scream that resounded through the house.

Kate met Maria on the run in the hallway, and the look of pure terror on her face was a reflection of her own. But before they reached the bedroom, they also heard the baby's sweet, wonderful cry, and knew the miracle had happened.

Weeping and speaking in Italian, Maria hurried into the room, leaving Kate to cling to the door frame on legs suddenly weak. Angelo had rolled up behind her in the wheelchair, and she stood aside to let him into the room.

Grinning from ear to ear, Michael held up the baby. "It's a boy," he announced. "A healthy boy, who all of a sudden decided he wasn't going to wait. He was breech, and that was the holdup. It was tough on mama and the baby, but they are going to be just fine."

It was nearly eight o'clock in the morning before things settled down. Michael tried to talk Maria into closing the store for the day, but she wouldn't hear of it. As it was, they were behind in the baking, and their friends and neighbors had to be told the good news.

"That's the real reason she's down there," Michael said later, while he and Kate were in the kitchen drinking a cup of coffee. "She's anxious to tell everyone the good news." He'd finally gotten Angelo into bed, and Trina and the baby were asleep. The baby's father was due in at noon, so everything was under control.

Except Kate's emotions. Inwardly, she was a wreck, and still filled with confusion.

Finally Michael said, "I owe you an explanation, but I'm not sure you'll understand. I'm not even sure if this is the right time, but we've been through too much together to hold back now.

"When I saw you on the plane, obviously in distress, the doctor in me made the initial contact. It wasn't that I didn't find you attractive, even beautiful, but the last thing I wanted to do was get involved with another beautiful, classy, glamorous woman. Monica was all those things, and she made my life hell. She liked the idea of being a doctor's wife, but she had her own idea of what a doctor should look like and how he should act. Well, that wasn't me, yet she insisted on trying to change me. When she couldn't, she broke the engagement and never looked back."

Kate shook her head. "I can understand how painful that must have been for you, but surely you don't think every woman who is beautiful and glamorous feels the same way."

Michael shrugged. "Maybe not. But when you've been hurt, you don't look for answers. You get on with your life, and try to forget. In any event, I had a meeting in L.A., and I planned to leave for Montana after that. It was going to be my first vacation in a long time, but then

I got a call from Maria. Angelo had had a dizzy spell, so I flew back to San Francisco, and you can take it from there."

Following along so far, and even understanding some of it, Kate said, "So why didn't you tell me you were a doctor?"

"I don't know. I almost told you in the cab that first day, but I didn't expect to see you again, so what was the point? And I probably wouldn't have seen you again, if our suitcases hadn't gotten switched. And to tell you the truth, I rather enjoyed playing the part of a rancher."

"Then you don't own a sheep ranch in Montana?"

"Oh, I own a sheep ranch, okay. I bought it for an investment, but I just haven't had the time to get up there to see it. This was my chance. I even bought the proper attire. Planned on looking and acting like 'Cowboy' Michael Gordon, and I knew I'd probably have the time of my life. A fantasy of sorts, I guess. Every little kid likes to play cowboy, and aren't all men little boys at heart? I have a married couple overseeing things, and a crew working the ranch. And my mother, who lives in Blue Sky, checks on things from time to time."

"And you live in San Francisco?"

"I have a house off Skyline Boulevard in Broadmoor. That's south of the city, near the ocean. I also have an apartment near the hospital, but no car here in the city. It's usually quicker to take a cab."

"And the Sea Nymph?"

"She's mine, but then you've probably guessed that by now."

"I suppose I should have guessed a lot of things. The signs were all there. Like all the western clothes in your suitcase that had never been worn, and the fact you'd heard of *Ms. California.* And your pager, your clean hands and manicured nails, and the fact that you knew all about boats."

"Well, the Sea Nymph has been my true friend, and she's gotten me through a lot of hard times. A place where I can go to sort out my problems, or simply kick back and rest if I've had a bad week."

Kate poured another cup of coffee and

walked to the window, looking out at the sea of rooftops. It was incredible, but his story wasn't all that different from her own. A fantasy had been the reason for her trip to San Francisco—the ultimate vacation.

"You don't know the whole truth about me either," she said finally.

He said, "And I suppose it begins with you giving me a wrong name?"

"It started long before that, Michael, when I was living in my hometown of Peach Springs, Arizona. Like I told you, I was engaged. Believe it or not, his name was Michael too. And he was a cattle rancher. He also believed a woman's place was in the home, and he refused to even consider letting me keep my job after we were married. Granted, my job wasn't much. Even though I'd gone to college, with a dream of becoming a journalist, there weren't any jobs in Peach Springs that needed my talents. So I got a job as a clerk in a store. And yes, I could have easily left it to be a full-time rancher's wife, but it was the principle of the thing. We had a lot of arguments, and he called my reasoning a bunch of 'women's-lib claptrap.' In the end, I broke our engagement and moved to L.A., where I could pursue my career, and hopefully find somebody to love who would respect me for who I am. And then, there you were on the plane. A tall, handsome cowboy, and exactly the kind of a man I'd walked away from two years earlier."

He looked at her levelly. "In a way, you're doing the same thing, Kate. You're lumping all cowboys into the same category. I'm not an authority, you understand, but don't you suppose there are a few of them around who might be more understanding?"

Kate sighed. "Of course there are, and my father is one of them. He's a wonderful man who has made my mother very happy. But you have to understand. I'd just spent a small fortune on this vacation, wanting it to be everything it could be, and that didn't include getting involved with a sheep rancher from Montana."

"So, how would you have reacted if I

had been wearing a suit, and told you I was a doctor?"

"Probably a lot differently. I'm sorry, Michael, but you asked."

Michael got up and put his coffee cup in the sink. "I'm sorry too, Katie lady. Now, if you'll excuse me, I'm going to check on Trina and the baby."

It was a dismissal, and she'd expected it, but it didn't ease the pain.

An hour later, after looking in on Trina and the baby, and giving her heartfelt thanks to Maria and Angelo for their hospitality, Kate took a cab to the airport. And once she was on the plane, she took out her notebook and made her last journal entry.

His name is Michael Gordon. I thought he was a sheep rancher from Montana, and now I wish he were. It would be so much easier knowing I'd fallen in love with a sheep rancher instead of a renowned San Francisco doctor who will probably never have a meaningful relationship because he's chasing after an illusion of what he wants a woman to be. But you see, I know what he wants, even if he doesn't. I saw the expression in his eyes when he was talking about Monica. He's looking for those same physical qualities again, and total glitz and glamor, only with a different attitude, and that isn't me. It can never be me. He liked what he saw on the plane that day, and pursued it, and now he realizes I wasn't that person at all. Well, I had a dream too, and now that dream is gone. And it's just as well.

Unaware that she had tears on her cheeks until she closed the journal, Kate turned toward the window and closed her eyes.

"Do you want to talk about it?" Angelo asked Michael later that evening. "Katherine has only been gone a few hours, and now you look like a man with a troubled heart."

They were sitting at the kitchen table

drinking coffee, and Michael took a deep breath. "I don't think talking about it is going to help, Angelo. I asked her a question, and she gave me the wrong answer."

"And what question was that?"

"Would she have been so cold and indifferent toward me that day on the plane, had she known I was a doctor? Her answer was no."

Angelo shook his head. "You knew she had a bad experience with the cowboy in Peach Springs, Arizona, so I would say her answer makes perfect sense. She didn't want to get involved with somebody like that man, any more than you wanted to get involved with somebody like Monica." Angelo lowered his voice. "Maria is in the next room watching TV, and I think it would be best if she doesn't hear this conversation. She is angry enough that you allowed Katherine to walk away so easily. If she knows you let her go simply because she didn't give you the answer you wanted to hear…."

"I had to let her go, to survive. When we were on the Sea Nymph, I knew it wasn't going to work. And it really didn't matter what approach I took."

"Then she didn't know you were a doctor."

"I know, and that's my point. Loving someone means accepting them as they are. As a cowboy, sheep rancher, or a doctor or a bum, for that matter. You fall in love with the person, not who or what they are."

Angelo threw up his arms. "You are turning things all around, my friend. So you might ask yourself this. What would have happened if Katherine really had been woman she was pretending to be?"

"I probably would've let her call a cab that day she came to exchange the suitcases, and that would have been the end of it. I wouldn't have tried to see her again."

"Without getting to know her? Because a woman happens to be beautiful and glamorous, does she automatically have to be like Monica? Listen to yourself, Michael. What's right for you shouldn't be right for her?"

Michael sighed. "I accused Kate of

doing the same thing, lumping people together when we are all individuals."

"Then perhaps you should consider that, and accept the fact you've been too harsh on Katherine, as well as yourself."

"If I've been harsh, it's because I had to be. More coffee?"

"I've had enough coffee, and I've had enough of your nonsense," Angelo almost shouted. "Katherine Callahan is a good woman, and you were a fool if you let her go.

Michael gave Angelo a wan smile. "You said the same thing about the last woman you tried to set me up with. Remember Delores, with the forty-six-inch hips?"

"Yes, but Katherine isn't Delores, or any of the other women who have passed through your life, and that includes Monica Lang."

Michael muttered, "I think you had better concentrate on getting well and being a new grandpa, and leave my heart to me, Angelo."

Angelo scoffed, "And so what are you doing about it? You have made one grand mess of things, and only you can straighten it out."

"I'm not going to do anything about it. I'm going to Blue Sky, Montana, and forget it ever happened. My flight leaves first thing in the morning."

Angelo shook his head. "You're making a big mistake, my friend, but I'm not about to waste my breath on a man who won't listen to reason, or who is blind to what we can all see. You arc afraid of falling in love again. And because of it, you've come up with all these sad excuses, instead of facing the truth."

Michael got to his feet, and scowled down at Angelo. "I think I'd better go, Angelo, before I say something I'll regret. You're a good friend, but it's my life, and nobody has the right to tell me how to live it. I'll spend the night at home, and go to the airport from there."

Angelo's answer was a heartfelt sigh, and Michael hurried out of the room.

Chapter Eight

"I guess this was a mistake too," Susan James said, eyeing Kate intently over the rim of her sunglasses. "And to tell you the truth, I've just about given up. You won't talk about your vacation, or tell me what's wrong, and now you're looking at that plate of sweet-and-sour pork like the cook at Wong's Palace laced it with poison. In the week since you've been home, I've tried in every way possible to put a smile on your face, and all I've gotten in return are frowns and grumbles. Even the gals in the office are beginning to talk, and you know how intense that can get. Poking and pointing, watercooler meetings, and a lot of big-time whispering."

They were sitting on Kate's little balcony, overlooking the flower-filled courtyard, and Kate tried for a smile. "I'm sorry, but it's just something I'd rather not talk about. That's a very pretty pink dress, by the way, and I like the way you've fixed your hair."

Susan ran a hand through her chestnut-colored hair and scowled. "Oh no you don't. You're not going to change the subject. You don't want to talk about 'it.' What is 'it,' Kate? Are you ill? You came to work last Monday looking like you'd just spent a week in an isolation cell at Tehachapi State Prison instead of a fun-filled week in romantic San Francisco, and you've been a million miles away ever since. You've lost weight, you have dark circles under your eyes, and you can forget the smile. That isn't a smile, it's a grimace. Well, if you're not going to eat all this marvelous Chinese, at least drink your wine."

Kate took a sip of wine. "I'm not ill,

Susan. I just haven't been sleeping well, that's all."

"And why is that? When I can't sleep, it usually means I'm having trouble with a boyfriend, or I'm behind on the rent, or I've gained ten pounds. Is that it? Did the trip cost more than you expected, and now you can't pay the rent?"

"Um, well, it was expensive, but I returned most of the clothes, and that lowered my credit card balances and gave me some extra cash."

Susan made a face. "Good grief, how did you manage that? I could understand it if you didn't wear the clothes, but—" Susan shoved her sunglasses up on her head. "Are you telling me you *didn't* wear all those beautiful clothes?"

Kate realized her mistake, and sighed. "I wore one dress on the flight up, but, well, then I lost my suitcase."

Susan filled her glass with wine, and took a healthy swallow. "Okay, let me get this straight. You called me from your hotel room that first night, remember? And I asked you if you were going to put on one of your knockout dresses and have dinner in one of the hotel's fabulous restaurants, or words to that effect. You told me you were feeling a little queasy from the flight, and were going to call room service. You didn't say one word about losing your luggage."

"I didn't lose my luggage. It was just one suitcase, and it wasn't actually lost. I mean, I got the wrong suitcase by mistake, that's all, but the whole thing was eventually straightened out."

"Uh-huh, so why do I get the feeling it's a lot more complicated than that? We've been good friends for two years, Kate. Sometimes I think you know more about me than I know about myself, and vice versa. But this time, you have me stumped. It's like you've pulled down some kind of a wall. A very secretive wall, I might add, and not even a sledgehammer is going to get through. I want to help, but how can I, when you won't let me in? Come on, Kate. What really happened in San Francisco?"

Kate sighed. "You know what they say. Truth is stranger than fiction. You wouldn't believe me if I told you."

"Oh, I don't know. Didn't I believe you that time you told me you knew how to rope a steer? And the time you told me Todd was going to ask me for a date? And how about that time you told me you were going to paint your bedroom walls lavender?" She waved a hand toward the apartment. "Well, your bedroom walls are lavender."

Kate was wearing a yellow terry caftan, and shoved her hands into the pockets. "I met a man on the flight to San Francisco...."

A smile spread across Susan's face. "Now we're getting somewhere!"

Although Kate only planned to give Susan a smattering of information, once she got started, she suddenly found herself pouring it all out. "I thought he was a sheep rancher from Montana, but he was really a doctor. We landed at San Francisco International in the middle of a storm, and had to share a cab into the city. Our luggage was similar, and when I found out I had the wrong suitcase, I thought he'd switched our suitcases so he'd have an excuse to see me later. Come to find out, it was an innocent mistake. He was going to bring my suitcase to the hotel, but I beat him to it. I knew he was staying with some people who owned a deli in North Beach, but I couldn't remember the name of it, or the address, only the street. I looked in the phone book, found a few listings, but not the cowboy. I looked up his name, and couldn't find that either. That's because he was listed in the yellow pages under 'physicians,' and not in the white pages. So, I took a cab to the street in North Beach, and lucked out. The bakery-deli was the first establishment I walked into. It was one I hadn't called, because I hadn't been looking under 'bakery.' "

When Kate stopped to take a breath, Susan took a deep breath too. "I think you'd better slow down, Kate. I'm still back with the guy you thought was a cowboy."

"Sorry."

"Don't be, and frankly, I'm in awe. So what happened after that?"

"We exchanged suitcases, and he took me back to the hotel. That night I went to dinner at the Tonga Room in the Fairmont Hotel."

"Alone?"

"Alone. It's really quite spectacular. Very tropical, and every hour, they have a storm over the pool. You can even feel the warm mist, though it doesn't actually get you wet, and all the lightning and thunder is thrilling. It's done with pipes, sound, and lighting, of course, but it's easy to forget it isn't real."

Susan frowned. "That sure doesn't sound like the kind of place where I'd want to dine alone."

"It wasn't. I realized that right after I got there. I'd been given a table near the pool, and was thinking about leaving when Michael showed up."

"Michael, the sheep rancher from Montana, who is really a doctor?"

"Yes, Michael Gordon. He's a San Francisco surgeon, who was in L.A. on business. From there, he was going on to Blue Sky, Montana to visit his mother and see his sheep ranch. But he had to go back to San Francisco, because he'd operated on the man who owns the deli, and Angelo had taken a turn for the worse."

"So, Michael Gordon *is* a sheep rancher."

"No, he isn't. He bought the ranch for an investment."

"Okay, so Michael shows up at the restaurant."

"Yes, and he told me he was there to meet some friends for a drink. But earlier, I'd mentioned I was going to have dinner there, so the whole thing was a ruse—his way of joining me for dinner."

"Why didn't he just ask you out to dinner?"

"Because he thought I might have a date. Anyway, when he found out I didn't have a date, he joined me. Needless to say, I was very pleased."

"Because now, you had a dinner partner, and wouldn't feel so out of place in such a romantic restaurant?"

"Yes, and because I wanted to be with Michael."

"Was he wearing cowboy clothes?"

"No, he was wearing a suit, and he looked wonderful. We had drinks and dinner, and made plans to be together the next day. He wanted to take me sight-seeing. We'd just finished dinner when his ex-fiancée happened by. I knew he'd been engaged, but I wasn't expecting somebody like Monica."

"Monica," Susan said a little wistfully. "Everybody I've known with that name is drop-dead gorgeous."

"And so is *this* Monica. She's a fashion model, and drips glamor. The kind of glamor I wanted to create when I bought all those fancy clothes."

"Okay, so you met his ex-fiancée. Then what?"

"Nothing. The evening ended, and I went to my room."

"And the next day, he took you sight-seeing?"

"No, because I changed my mind. I left him a note at the hotel desk, telling him I was going home."

"You were going to cut your vacation short?"

"That was my plan."

"Care to tell me why?"

"It's too involved."

"And your story isn't?"

"I told you, you wouldn't believe it."

"Well, I'm still listening."

"When I left the hotel to get a cab to go to the airport, Michael was there with three dozen red roses and a limo. I thought he wanted to take me to the airport, but instead, we went to his boat. Of course, I didn't know it was his boat at the time. He said he wanted to talk, yet he kept putting it off. He had the salon filled with flowers, and champagne on ice.... While I was in the head—that's the rest room—he went to the boat shop to make a phone call. That's when I decided to leave. I knew going to the boat with him was a mistake. I was going to find a pay phone along Marina Boulevard and call a cab, but I only got as far as the gangplank. That's when I tripped and went overboard."

Susan sucked in her breath. "You fell overboard?"

"Yes, and Michael saved my life. I was still a little light-headed from my fall, and he didn't want me to be alone, so I spent the night with the Boninis, the people who own the deli. That's when I found out Michael was a doctor. During the night, the Boninis' daughter Trina, who was very, very pregnant, went into labor, and Michael delivered the baby. The next morning, I caught a flight home. It wasn't until I was in the air that I remembered all my underwear and nightclothes were still on the boat."

Susan grinned mischievously. "Well, I'm not going to touch that one with a ten-foot pole."

"It's not what you think, Susan. When I fell overboard, one of my suitcases went with me, and everything got wet. Thank goodness it wasn't the suitcase with all my good clothing."

Dazed, Susan could only stare at Kate, and it was a long minute before she said, "You're right. I don't believe it. Good grief, Kate, that sounds like something right out of a romantic comedy! A farce!"

"I know, but remember, you're the one who asked."

"Uh-huh, and now you can tell me what you're holding back, because it certainly doesn't sound like something that would cause all this gloom and depression. Mercy! You had a real, honest-to-goodness romantic adventure, and that would sure put a smile on my face!"

"But don't you see, Susan? I can't smile, because somewhere along the line, I managed to fall in love."

Susan groaned. "Uh-oh. I should have guessed, though for the life of me, I can't possibly see where you had time. Not that I don't believe in love at first sight, but you were so…so busy! And I take it Michael doesn't feel the same way about you?"

"To be honest, I don't know how he feels. Our whole relationship was a charade from the beginning. Like a masquerade ball. There I was, with a beautiful wardrobe, staying at the Fairmont Hotel, pretending to be somebody I wasn't. And there he was, dressed in jeans and cowboy boots, pretending to be a sheep rancher. He'd gotten badly hurt by glamorous Monica, and wanted no part of me. And because I thought he was a sheep rancher, which is exactly the kind of guy I walked away from two years ago, I wanted no part of him. At least that's the way it was in the beginning."

"But surely, when you found out the truth about each other, that changed things."

"It should have, but it didn't. I think it probably made it worse, if anything. Especially when I realized that Monica is exactly the kind of woman he's still looking for, no matter what he says. He's a brilliant surgeon, a part of San Francisco's elite, so what would he want with the likes of me?"

"That's foolish, Kate, and don't you dare sell yourself short like that. You're a beautiful woman, with a whole lot to offer."

"Beautiful? Except for the short time on the plane, and that night at dinner, he saw me at my worst, Susan. And I cringe every time I think about it."

"You'd be beautiful wearing a gunnysack, Kate."

Kate got up and stood at the railing, trying to gather some warmth from the sun. "That last time we were together, when he knew I was going to take the next available flight home, if he'd said something.... If he had given me one tiny shred of hope, I would have stayed. But he didn't even say good-bye. It was like circumstances had thrown us together, he'd gotten stuck with me because of it, and finally, he was getting me out of his hair. On one hand, my heart was breaking, but on the other hand, I couldn't wait to get away from him."

Susan moved to the railing, and gave Kate a hug. "The human heart can be pretty powerful, Kate. It can love and feel pain, and rebound quite easily. All it takes is time. I'm truly sorry your vacation was ruined, and you had to go through that heartbreaking ordeal, but talking about it is the first step to recovery. And each day will get a little better. You haven't said what he looks like."

Kate closed her eyes. "He's very tall and sinewy, with wide shoulders. His hair is dark and wavy, and his eyes are cornflower blue. He has beautiful teeth, a slightly crooked smile, and two elongated dimples. At first, I thought one of them was a scar, but it wasn't. He's also very tan, and has long fingers—the fingers of a surgeon."

"He sounds gorgeous."

"He is. And he could have his pick of dozens of beautiful, glamorous women."

"But he picked you."

"No, he didn't. I just 'happened,' Susan. 'It' just happened. A chain of events that were played out until the end. And it ended the only way it could have."

"I don't buy that for a minute, Kate. What you've described to me are two people who were sending out mixed signals the whole time they were together. And here's something else—You left a note for him, telling him you were going home. So why the limo and the red roses? Why did he take you to his boat so you could 'talk'?"

Kate sighed. "I've asked myself that question a dozen times, and I truly don't know, because we never got the chance to talk."

"Did it ever occur to you he didn't want you to leave, and he thought by showering you with a little romance, you might change your mind?"

"So I could do what? Spend the rest of my vacation with him? We're only talking about a few more days, and he knew my home was here in L.A., and that I had a job waiting for me, so what could be accomplished in a couple of days?"

"Maybe a lot, Kate, if you guys had given it half a chance."

Kate was searching for a response to that, when the doorbell rang. "I'm not expecting anybody, and I'm not dressed."

"Relax, Kate, I'll get it," Susan said, hurrying into the apartment.

Kate sat down at the table, and closed her eyes. She could hear the murmur of voices, but couldn't hear the words. Nor did she care. It was Saturday. Mrs. Anderson across the hall was home, and probably needed to borrow something. Or it might be the paperboy. It was the first of the month....

"You'd feel a lot better if you opened your eyes," the husky voice said. "And you might consider sucking on some crushed ice. Your friend said you weren't feeling well...."

With her heart beating wildly in her

chest, Kate stared up at Michael. And when she could untangle her tongue, she managed to sputter, "W-what are you doing here?"

"Brought you this," he said, folding himself into the chair across from her.

Kate took the bag and looked inside. It was her underwear and nightclothes.

"I was going to put them in a box and mail them to you, but I decided to bring them down instead."

"How did you get my address?"

"I have friends at the hotel." He motioned toward the apartment. "Nice apartment. Feminine, but with a lot of punch. It's what I expected."

"Susan, my friend—"

"She gave me the thumb's-up sign, and said to tell you she'd call you later." He nodded at the table. "Looks like I interrupted lunch."

Michael was wearing white slacks, and a blue shirt the color of his eyes, and although he was still the handsomest man she'd ever seen, he looked haggard, like he hadn't gotten much sleep either.

"We were finished with lunch. If you're hungry…."

He shook his head. "I haven't had much appetite lately. The Boninis send their love."

"And the baby?"

"He's beautiful, and healthy. They've named him Robert Michael."

"Did you ever get to Blue Sky?"

"I did. I only stayed a couple of days, but I enjoyed every minute of it. It's beautiful country. Wide open and free. There was still some snow on the ground, but it didn't prohibit me from learning to ride a horse."

"Then you got to play cowboy?"

"I did, and I have the battle scars to prove it." He held up his hands. "I'd been there a full day before I realized why all the ranch hands were wearing gloves."

Kate looked at his bruised and scraped hands, and took a deep breath. "You know, I noticed your hands on the plane that day. They weren't the hands of a cowboy."

Michael leaned back in the chair. "I noticed your eyes. I thought they were the most beautiful color green I'd ever seen."

Kate cocked her head. "I had my eyes closed most of the time, and you said you noticed I was ill, and the doctor in you wanted to come to my rescue."

"That too."

She said "Michael" and he said "Kate" at the same time, and they both smiled. She said, "You go first."

"I think we should talk."

Kate nodded. "I know."

"And I don't want to talk about politics, or religion, or the economy, or the weather, or the price of tea in China. I want to talk about us, Kate. I want to start over from the beginning, and I want to tell you the truth."

"Is this the same conversation we were supposed to have on your boat?"

"Yes and no. I've had some time to think. I might not have been totally honest with you that day on the boat, but I will be now. And that's what this is all about, honesty.

"The only thing I had on my mind that day on the plane was my concern for Angelo, and getting to San Francisco as quickly as possible. But the inebriated passenger sitting beside me wasn't making it easy. I saw the empty seat across the aisle, and moved. And that was when I realized you were ill. Later, after I dropped you off at the hotel, I also realized I was attracted to you, and it was disconcerting to say the least, because Monica had put me through hell, and the last thing I wanted was to become involved with another beautiful, glamorous woman. But there was something about you that didn't ring true."

Kate gave a heartfelt sigh. "That's because I was only pretending to be a glitzy, glamorous woman."

"I know, and I think I knew it all the time. But that left me with a couple of unanswered questions. First of all, why would a beautiful woman in her own right pretend to be something she wasn't? And the biggie—would you have been so cold and indifferent toward me if I'd been wearing a suit on the plane, and had introduced myself as a doctor?"

"You asked me that question the morning I left San Francisco, Michael."

"Yes, I did, and you answered me. It wasn't the answer I wanted to hear, Kate. It told me that being a cowboy, or in this case, a sheep rancher, wasn't good enough for you. I tried to put it into perspective, because I knew you'd been badly hurt by that guy in Arizona, but it didn't work. It was the Monica scenario all over again. I don't think she ever loved me, but she loved the idea of being a doctor's wife. Unfortunately, even before I decided to go 'western' and head for Montana, I still didn't conform to her standards. My life-style is casual. I'm more comfortable in jeans and slacks than a suit. I drive a ten-year-old car, my house needs a coat of paint, and sometimes I forget to get a haircut."

Kate looked at the sadness in his eyes, and took a deep breath. "I thought you'd lost interest in me when you found out I wasn't like Monica. And as to the first part of your question, I told you all about my disastrous relationship with Michael Downs, which was the reason I didn't want anything to do with a cowboy. I also told you my vacation was no more than a fantasy."

"I know, and that's why I think we should stop deceiving ourselves, and lay it out. I've just gone through the worst week of my life, Katie lady, because I let the woman I love walk away. No, don't say anything. Let me finish, and then if you want to kick me out. I'll go.

"I love you, Kate Callahan. I think I fell in love with you that day on the plane. I've been fighting it, and I've refused to listen to what everybody has been trying to tell me. And I've been getting it from all directions. Angelo and Maria are hardly speaking to me, my friends think I'm an idiot for letting you go, and even my mother read me the riot act. But it wasn't until yesterday that I realized I couldn't go on without facing it, and you. I've never been good with words, but…."

With tears in her eyes, Kate reached across the table and took his hand. And when she spoke, the words came straight from her heart. "I'm in love with you too,

Michael. But I've been fighting it, because I didn't think you could possibly be interested in somebody like me. You've seen the real me. And I'm not that lady on the plane, who was pretending to be somebody she wasn't, and could never be. If I were a different kind of woman and maybe a little more sure of myself, I would have been able to start a first-rate campaign to 'catch the handsome doctor.' But I've never been good at flirting, I don't know the first thing about setting a man-trap, and I've never been good at playing games. At least not when it comes to human emotions. So, what you see is what you get."

With a groan, Michael stood up and pulled Kate into his arms. "I fell in love with all those qualities you just described. You have a natural beauty that shines from within. And you have more spunk and backbone that twenty women put together. You also have one great body. I've had dreams about that body, I can tell you—the kinds of dreams that have sent me running for a cold shower.

I've done a lot of fighting with myself over it, over us."

Kate snuggled against him, burying her face against the warmth of his chest. The smell was familiar—Ivory soap and musk—and she closed her eyes. "My legs are too long."

His chuckle was warm. "No way. Your legs are perfect just the way they are, along with the rest of you."

"I didn't want to leave that day, Michael. If you had given me even the slightest hint about how you felt…."

"But that was the problem," he said, raining sweet kisses over her face. "I didn't know how I felt. I couldn't stand the thought of you leaving either, but I couldn't ask you to stay."

"And now?"

"I want you to marry me. I know I haven't the right to ask you to give up your career and move to San Francisco, but I shouldn't have any trouble getting a position at a hospital down here."

Kate looked up at him with stars in her eyes. "You'd do that for me?"

"And a whole lot more."

Kate shook her head. “I couldn’t let you do that, Michael, but I know for a fact that *Ms. California* plans on opening an office in San Francisco. I could be a part of that opening.”

“Is that a yes?” he asked huskily.

“Oh, yes! I’ll marry you! Yes, yes, yes!”

“And those are the words I’ve been waiting to hear,” he said, burying his face against her hair.

Epilogue

Kate stood on the deck of the Sea Nymph, wrapped in one of Michael's robes, and watched the sun rise in the east. An offshore breeze had kept the fog from rolling in, and there was every indication it was going to be a beautiful summer day.

"Even the weather is cooperating," Michael said, walking up behind her. "The trip up the coast should be spectacular."

"We could still fly to Hawaii for our honeymoon…."

"And have you sick the whole way? Touring the northern coast in the Sea

Nymph is a much better idea, sweetheart, and it really doesn't matter where we go, as long as we're together. The coffee is ready, Mrs. Gordon."

She leaned against him, marveling at the feel of his arms around her. They'd gotten married yesterday, in front of family and friends—his and hers—and they'd spent the night making love, discovering love, and talking, yet now she could only murmur, "I want you, Michacl…."

His arms tightened. "You have me, Kate. Now and forever. I'll never let you go."

Kate smiled, thinking about her long-awaited fantasy vacation, and how things had turned out. Sometimes the fears that kept people apart were the ones that made them the most alike and, eventually, with a little bit of luck, brought them together. Now, the future would be theirs to share.

"I love you," she said, wrapping her arms around him.

"Hmm, me too. Let's have some coffee, and then I'll show you how much."

Made in the USA
Monee, IL
07 September 2026

62521453R00109